# "Paul is closer to me than I ever will be to you."

The surprising words got Missy's attention. She stopped in her tracks, but didn't turn around. She could feel a rush of adrenaline zip through her body from head to toe.

"Paul knew you for a couple years," Missy brought Mashela up to date. "But Paul and I are *covenant brother and sister.* You probably don't understand exactly what that means, but basically it means we're closer than you'll ever hope to be. Sorry to burst your bubble." Missy started again for the door.

"Apparently you forget how excited he was to see me." Missy stopped again and turned around. Mashela was standing now, with a bluish cast on her body from the light blue force field she stood behind. Missy scowled.

"Yep, he was pretty excited to see me," Mashela repeated, looking around her cell as though her thoughts were elsewhere. "In fact, I'd say he's spent more time talking to me the past few weeks than he's spent talking to you. Coming in the evenings to talk about old times, the fun we've had together..."

"Oh, please. Get over yourself."

Mashela smiled. "Oh, I'm sorry. Did I strike a nerve, Miss Ashton? Golly, looks like you have a rival."

Missy shrugged her shoulders. "You're not much of a rival," she noted. "After all,"—Missy waved her forefinger in Mashela's direction—"you're the one in a cage."

Mashela peered at Missy, her brown eyes glaring out from beneath low eyebrows. She smiled maliciously.

"Famous last words," she whispered.

**Look for these other books in the *Commander Kellie and the Superkids*<sub>SM</sub> Series!**

#1 — *The Mysterious Presence*
#2 — *The Quest for the Second Half*
#3 — *Escape From Jungle Island*
#4 — *In Pursuit of the Enemy*
#5 — *Caged Rivalry*
#6 — *Mystery of the Missing Junk*

*Commander Kellie and the Superkids*<sub>SM</sub>

**#5**

# Caged Rivalry

*Christopher P.N. Maselli*

**Harrison House**
Tulsa, Oklahoma

*Caged Rivalry*
ISBN 1-57794-231-0            30-0905
Copyright © 2001 by Kenneth Copeland Ministries
Fort Worth, Texas 76192-0001

Published by Harrison House, Inc.
P.O. Box 35035
Tulsa, Oklahoma 74153

## Dedication

For anyone who has
ever had their
hand in a cage...

# Contents

| | | |
|---|---|---|
| *Prologue: Letter From Missy* | | 9 |
| 1 | A Subtle Beginning | 13 |
| 2 | Unequally Yoked | 29 |
| 3 | Breakout | 41 |
| 4 | Small Discoveries | 51 |
| 5 | Her Secret Past | 65 |
| 6 | Track Down | 73 |
| 7 | Arrival of the Serfsled | 87 |
| 8 | The Ring | 97 |
| 9 | The Cost of Offense | 109 |
| | *Epilogue: The Great Bargain* | 125 |

Hey Superkid,

My name is Missy Ashton. And I have a story that I'm sure you'll love—because it's all about me! [Hee-hee! ☺] Though this story is full of all the fun I bring to Superkid Academy, it's also a very serious one.

Now let me just take a moment here to tell you that Superkid Academy is where I live right now. It's kind of like a school, only way better because, sure, we learn about math and English and stuff, but we also learn about the latest survival techniques and, most importantly, God's Word, which is the best thing. Is that a run-on sentence? Hmmm...I'd better study my grammar better.

Anyway, Superkid Academy is where my friends and I in the Blue Squad are training. The Blue Squad consists of me, Paul, Rapper, Valerie, Alex and Techno. Techno's just a robot, but he's still part of the team. Of course, there's also our fearless leader, Commander Kellie. Together, the seven of us seem to keep jumping into one adventure after another—but we always adventure with God, which is the best!

Believe me, I know what I'm talking about—and you'll see why I say it's serious. Because you're about to find out how I tried to have an adventure without God—and what it cost me. [Note: Do not attempt this at home.]

Check it out—you'll see. Going with God is the only way to go!!

Missy

# Caged Rivalry

# A Subtle Beginning

The door to the holding room buzzed softly as it slid open. A young guard stationed outside stepped aside to allow Missy entrance.

This wasn't her favorite place.

This wasn't her favorite person.

But bringing a meal to the lawbreaker was Missy's responsibility tonight...and *every* Thursday night until the young, female captive was brought to trial. Until then, the commanders at the Academy had agreed to hold her. They did it for her safety—they knew transporting such a highly sought prisoner anywhere else was a risk to her...and it was a risk to Superkid Academy should she see its secret location. If her old employer, Notoriously Malicious Enterprises (NME), ever discovered Superkid Academy was secretly located in one of NME's old buildings, trouble with a capital "T" would be storming the Academy's gates.

NME's sole mission was to rule the world, one deceived child at a time. Superkid Academy's mission, on the other hand, was to save the world, one saved child at a time. Their missions conflicted, and if NME ever had the opportunity at an upper hand, they'd take it—working to destroy Superkid Academy in the process.

For a while, this young, beautiful prisoner *was* their upper hand. But through a series of recent circumstances, she had been captured and was waiting to be brought to justice. That thought pleased Missy.

The prisoner practically asked for the ruling that was sure to come her way. The Superkids met her five weeks ago when she tried to extract secret information from Alex Taylor, one of the Blue Squad members and one of Missy's friends. This prisoner lied to Alex, threatened him, beat him up and actually tried to kill him...but what she hadn't counted on was the power of God coming on the scene. Needless to say, Alex had since recovered— and here she was, not looking so tough now in Superkid Academy's holding area.

The room was nearly silent, save the buzzing of the round, fluorescent ceiling lights and the soft drone of several electrical climate units placed around the room. The only other sound was a small medband on the prisoner's wrist, quietly beeping with every heartbeat, ready to alert medical staff if her health was compromised.

On the other side of a light blue electronic field, the young, dark-skinned captive's eyelids opened slowly, parting her soft eyelashes.

"Morning," she whispered. Her voice was slightly hoarse.

"Actually, it's afternoon," Missy corrected. The captive rolled her eyes and then cleared her throat.

"Doesn't make much difference when you don't see daylight," she quickly responded, sitting up on the cot where she slept. She yawned and stretched. She wore a fluorescent-orange and black uniform for easy identification as a prisoner. Through deliberate holes, a metal card was sewn into the right chest pocket of her shirt. It read:

## NME AGENT #2039
## MASHELA KNAVERY
## SKA 5-462-88-7

Mashela Knavery. A highly decorated NME agent known as sheer trouble. Conniving, conspiring, controlling trouble.

"You're in here for the trouble you caused," Missy said flatly, avoiding eye contact. The blonde reached down to slide open a small, metal door that led into the cramped chamber. Mashela grabbed the knob on the other side and held it closed. Missy tugged at it and then looked at Mashela.

"What? You don't want your food?"

"I want you to answer a question first," Mashela responded. Missy stayed quiet, looking at her warily. Neither girl let go of the door. Mashela continued, "You hate me, don't you?"

"The Superkid Manual—the Bible—says to love your enemies."

"You didn't answer the question."

"I don't *hate* you."

"Well, I can tell you don't *love* me."

Missy looked down at the covered, plastic plate she was holding. With a film of fine droplets, steam had coated the inside of the clear, plastic cover, hiding the spaghetti and vegetables underneath.

"Look, I've got things to do," Missy stated, looking away. "Do you want your food or not?"

Mashela leaned back and let go. Missy slid open the small door and shoved in the warm, plastic plate she had brought down.

Without warning, Mashela lashed out and grabbed Missy's right hand. Missy dropped the plate straight down onto the cot. It bounced lightly. Missy nearly screamed, but suddenly realized the most Mashela could do would be to slap her wrist with a wet spaghetti noodle...or at worst, she might break the included, flimsy, plastic spork on the back of her hand.

"What do you think you're doing?" Missy asked, staring straight into Mashela's brown eyes. They met Missy's baby blues.

"I knew Paul before you did."

Mashela mentioning Paul's name made Missy uneasy. Paul West, another of the five Superkids on the Blue Squad, was a close friend of Missy's and hearing his name on Mashela's lips was like hearing it hissed from the mouth of a snake.

"So what if you knew Paul before me," Missy admitted. "Big whoop."

"Paul tells me you're his sister."

Mashela knew more than she was letting on. Missy decided to play along. "That's right...Paul's dad and mine were best friends, covenant brothers. The way we figure it, that makes Paul and me covenant brother and sister as well."

"Oh, so you're not *really* brother and sister."

"No...but because we didn't have any brothers or sisters, we saw this as God kind of giving us each other as a family. So, no, we're not brother and sister by flesh and blood, but—" Missy paused. "Why am I telling you this? What's your point?"

Mashela's eyes grew wide. "You don't know Paul like I do."

"Let go."

*"You don't know him like I do."*

"Let go!" Missy jerked her arm back and skinned her thumb on the metal door. "Ouch!"

Mashela threw her head back and laughed. Missy just stared at her and rubbed her thumb.

"You are one kid desperately in need of some help from above," Missy whispered, shaking her head.

The young girl behind the field stopped laughing and looked straight at Missy again. "Oh, I'm just giving you a hard time," she said lightly. "I think it's funny. You're so predictable. You and I are totally alike."

The shock on Missy's face was evident. "Scuse me?"

"You heard me. We're the same. Look at us."

Missy frowned. She touched her skinned thumb to her lips.

"We both recently became teenagers," Mashela explained. "Neither of us grew up with brothers or sisters. We're both beautiful..."

"Well, *one* of us is anyway," Missy interjected.

"Thank you."

Missy looked down at Mashela. "I was talking about me." She smiled curtly. Mashela Knavery smiled back.

"Well, what else do we have in common?" Missy asked playfully, flipping her long, curly hair back with a toss of her head. "Let's see...you're a weapons special-ist and highly trained in covert maneuvers for NME. Now how am I like that again? I forget..."

Mashela continued smiling. She seemed to be enjoying their conversation. "What we've learned is different," Mashela admitted. "But you, my dear, are a highly trained Superkid. I've done my homework. And I know we've both worked hard for our training. So you see, in a way, we *are* alike."

Missy stayed silent.

"Although," Mashela taunted, "I do have several strengths you don't have."

"Oh, really?"

"Yes, really. For instance, I don't have a family I'm all gushy-gushy worried about. That makes me strong."

"Hardly," Missy countered. "A family *brings* you strength, Mashela."

"Difference number two: I have incredible wit and cunning."

"Oh, and she's humble, too!" Missy announced to no one in particular. "Well, what you're calling 'wit and cunning' most would categorize as deceitfulness. But either way, I have the Word of God."

"So we're evenly matched on that one."

"Evenly matched?! I think I'll stick with the Word."

"We'll see where that gets you."

Missy nodded confidently, smiling tightly.

"So you're saying we are equally matched for strengths?" Missy asked rhetorically. "Well, I'd say we have quite a few differences."

"For instance, I knew Paul before you did."

"Which brings us full circle. Now if you'll excuse me—" Missy turned to leave.

"Paul's closer to me than he ever will be to you." The surprising words got Missy's attention. She stopped in her tracks, but didn't turn around. She could feel a rush of adrenaline zip through her body from head to toe.

"Paul knew you for a couple years," Missy brought Mashela up to date. "But Paul and I are *covenant brother and sister.* You probably don't understand exactly what that means, but basically it means we're closer than you'll ever hope to be. Sorry to burst your bubble." Missy started again for the door.

"Apparently you forget how excited he was to see me." Missy stopped again and turned around. Mashela was standing now, with a bluish cast on her body from the light blue force field. Missy scowled.

It was true. Paul had been pretty thrilled to see Mashela, his old buddy from Sawyer Orphanage with whom he had lost contact. Missy had cast it off as no big deal. Now that Paul knew Mashela was an NME agent, he realized she had changed over the years, didn't he?

"Yep, he was pretty excited to see me," Mashela repeated, looking around her cell as though her thoughts were elsewhere. "In fact, I'd say he's spent more time talking to me the past few weeks than he's spent talking to you. Coming in the evenings to talk about old times, the fun we've had together..."

"Oh, please. Get over yourself."

Mashela smiled. "Oh, I'm sorry. Did I strike a nerve, Miss Ashton? Golly, looks like you have a rival."

Missy shrugged her shoulders. "You're not much of a rival," she noted. "After all,"—Missy waved her forefinger in Mashela's direction—"you're the one in a cage."

Mashela peered at Missy, her brown eyes glaring out from beneath low eyebrows. She smiled maliciously.

"Famous last words," she whispered.

▲   ▲   ▲

"That girl gives me the creeps," Missy admitted to her roommate and close friend, Valerie Rivera. Their bedroom was dark and across the room a digital clock glowed "10:06 p.m." The two friends regularly went to sleep around 10 since they had to be up early the next morning for devotions, training exercises, classes and more.

Superkid Academy was their training ground for reaching the world. The schedule was rigorous at times, but the training always made it worth their while. Not only did they grow physically and intellectually, but also spiritually. With the bases covered, by graduation, they would be ready to impact their world like never before.

Missy and Valerie were both in the Academy's prestigious Blue Squad with three boys—Paul, Rapper and Alex—a robot, Techno, and their leader—Commander Kellie. It was the kind of team most groups could only hope to have. Together, they were a cord that could not be broken.

"She certainly needs Jesus," Valerie agreed. "But she also needs us to shine His Light to her."

"I guess."

"You don't sound convinced."

Missy reached out in the dark, over and behind her head. She felt for the metal lamp on the corner table between the heads of the beds. When her fingertip touched the cool lamp, the room was flooded with brilliant light.

Valerie's eyes shot open, then closed, and the 11-year-old brunette ducked under her covers on instinct.

"Ugh! Missy! Turn it off!"

Missy was facing Valerie and squinting, but her eyes soon adjusted. "I know she needs Jesus, but she still gives me the creeps. It's like she's got something against me. I think it has to do with Paul."

Valerie popped up a corner of her blue bedsheet and squinted out at Missy. "You couldn't tell me that with the light *off?*"

"No, Val, this is serious," Missy pouted. Valerie pulled her covers back down from her head. Her thin, naturally pretty face was accented by shadows cast from the bright light. She propped herself up on one elbow and pulled her straight, dark brown hair back with her other hand. Her brown eyes stayed squinted.

"Wanna talk about it?" Valerie offered.

Missy sat up and adjusted her white pajamas. She ran her cherry red fingernails through the ends of her long, blond hair.

"Well..." prompted Valerie.

"I don't know what to say," said Missy. "I feel bad for feeling this way, but after what she said, I can't help it."

"What did she say to you?"

Missy tightened her eyes and took a deep breath, then opened them and stared ahead. "She said she knew Paul before I did."

"Well...she did. That's no crime."

"I guess." Missy turned back to Valerie. "And she kept comparing herself to me. In one breath, she said we were the same and then in another she boasted that she was far superior. My contentment isn't based on what she thinks, but..."

Valerie listened.

"Then she brought everything back to Paul and made it seem like our covenant brother/sister relationship wasn't worth pig mud."

"Did you just say, *'pig mud'?*"

"Well…"

"Look, I'd expect nothing less from her," Valerie surmised. "She's proven herself to be a liar. That's part of the reason she's here."

"I know. But it just made me uncomfortable. Paul's a good friend, and I really see our covenant brother/sister relationship as a blessing from God. Paul needed a family and we were there for him. And, in a way, since my brother, Scott, died, my parents have wanted a boy they could bless like they've blessed me. And, you know…" Missy picked at some lint on her comforter, "I like the idea of having someone who's like a brother, too. Someone who's like part of the family whom I can go to for advice."

Valerie nodded after a short pause. "You know I'm always here for you, don't you?"

Missy looked over at Valerie who was still squinting.

"You're a great friend, Val," Missy smiled, "and you always will be. You know me better than just about anyone else. So you know what I mean, don't you? I've just always wanted a brother."

"God's blessed you." Valerie yawned and then giggled. "Oh, I'm sorry. I'm a little tired."

Missy giggled, too. She held her skinned thumb up in the light. "Look what that girl did to me!" she shouted, laughing. "She inflicted a wound! Oh no! Call the medics!"

The girls began to laugh. "You are so goofy after bedtime," Valerie managed to say before breaking up again.

"A wound! A wound!" Missy was shouting, holding her thumb up in the air. "I've been inflicted with a wound!"

"Well, if that's the worst Mashela does to you, you have nothing to be concerned about," Valerie added.

Missy chuckled again. "Well, it will be," she stated seriously. "I'm not going to let her get to me. She may have covert training, weapons training, potty training, whatever. But I'm a Superkid and I have God's Word. And I know He can even heal this little wound!"

"A-men!" punctuated Valerie. "Now it's time for you to go to sleep before you keep us both up all night laughing."

The girls lay back down and Missy reached over to turn off the light. Before she did, she thrust her thumb out to Valerie once more.

"A wound!" she exclaimed. Valerie giggled, trying to give her roommate a serious look.

"Go to sleep!"

"A wound!"

"Go to sl—Missy, where's your ring?"

Smiling, Missy turned her right hand with the wounded thumb around. "It's right—" Suddenly her eyes grew large. *"Where's my ring?!"*

Missy felt around her finger, tangibly verifying it was missing as she looked around her bedcovers.

"Did I have it when I came in the room tonight?"

"I don't know...where were you last?"

"I've been *everywhere* today—all our regular classes, in the...oh!...Mashela!"

"Now don't jump to conclusions. You could have lost it anywhere."

"Val, that creepy girl distracted me by grabbing my hand and then took it off. I was so concerned about my thumb and what she was saying I didn't even notice."

"Are you sure? But why would she want your ring?" Valerie wondered.

Missy's earlier laughter had now turned into anger. She threw off her rumpled covers and jumped out of bed.

"She wanted my ring because she knows Paul gave it to me as a symbol of our covenant relationship. She's trying to get under my skin!"

"Well, you're blessed," Valerie stated flatly. "Luke 6 says when people hate you and are cruel to you, you can be happy because God has great things in store for you."

"In that case, I oughta be thrilled. This girl's a real piece of work. Val, do you remember when Paul gave that ring to me?"

Valerie nodded with a look of concern on her face.

A sweet memory flashed through Missy's mind as she thought back to that occasion. It had happened a little over five weeks ago, the day after Paul discovered who his parents had been. They were staying at Missy's parents' house and when Missy awoke the next morning, she discovered Paul was nowhere to be found.

Four hours later, Paul came hopping up the concrete steps to the Ashton's front door and greeted Missy with a closed fist. Missy pulled his fingers open, and to her surprise, in his palm was a simple silver ring that fit her finger perfectly. Even now she could remember the words he had said:

"Missy, as the daughter of my dad's covenant brother, I just wanted you to know I'm proud to be in covenant with your family. I'm proud to have your parents as friends who care for me and have promised to be there for me. And I'm proud to have a covenant sister who will always be a friend to me." It was sweet, formal and even kind of poetic...just what she had always imagined a brother to be like. She accepted the ring and hadn't taken it off for any reason.

Now it had been stolen.

Yep, she was *real* happy.

Missy moved to the dresser on the other side of the small room and tapped a touchpad on the front of the bottom, right-hand drawer. It quickly slid open with a soft, whooshing sound. She reached in and pulled out the top ensemble—her workout clothes. It was a feathered-gray sweat shirt and matching sweat pants. Her name was embroidered in blue thread on the front of the shirt. She threw it on top of her pajamas in an instant.

"Father God," Valerie prayed behind her, "we stand on Your Word in Isaiah 54:17 and believe that no weapon formed against Missy will prevail tonight and every accusing word that rises up against her will fail. Father, You said in James 1:5 that if we ask for wisdom You will give it to us. Well, I pray for wisdom for Missy tonight as she talks to Mashela. In Jesus' Name. Amen."

"Isn't that just like the devil?" Missy said, standing at the door. "He sees a blessing God has given you, lets you enjoy it and then subtly tries to take it away."

Valerie nodded.

"Well, not this time," Missy stated matter-of-factly. "I'm going to go claim what's mine."

As the lift zipped up a floor, Missy prayed quietly under her breath. She prayed for courage and prayed that Mashela would "fess up" to her crime. She'd had enough of Mashela's empty words and hollow threats. She just wanted what belonged to her. For a brief moment, she felt relief that the troublemaker was stationed behind electronic bars. She could only imagine what Alex had gone through with her on the loose.

The lift door opened with a hiss and Missy exited, her bare feet receiving chills from the smooth cement floor. As she walked, she pulled her hair back into a ponytail and snapped a fluffy, blue scrunchie around its base. She wasn't all "fixed up" like usual, but who would see her anyway? She walked down the hall determined. The young guard outside the holding room glanced up at her arrival and nodded. Missy smiled and he stepped aside, allowing her entrance. The door hissed open. She stepped inside and immediately froze, staring ahead in shock.

Mashela was there, behind the light blue force field, sitting up on her cot. But what shocked Missy wasn't Mashela. It was the young visitor sitting, relaxed, on the floor in front of her, conversing...and laughing. It was Paul.

Missy wondered for a second if she had just stepped into a bad, late-night pizza dream. But, no, it was Paul's unmistakable frame sitting there. He wore a red rugby and jeans. He ran his hands through his short, blond hair, then leaned back on them. He hadn't noticed her arrival.

The captured NME agent spied Missy out of the corner of her eye, but didn't acknowledge her. Instead, she grew louder.

"Oh, Pauly, you're *so* funny! We sure had some great times together when we were at the orphanage. You remember the time we sneaked out at night without Gran knowing and broke into Old Man Myer's house—"

Paul leaned forward in a chuckle. "Oh, yeah, yeah— and we turned all his furniture upside down while he was asleep! I still think maybe we shouldn't have turned over the fishbowl, though."

Missy was gaping. She folded her arms across her chest and walked across the back of the room.

"The funniest thing was the next day, though," Mashela added enthusiastically. "He was so mad and had no clue who pulled the prank. Then you go up to the old man and offer to put everything back in place—"

"For a small fee," Paul pointed out. The two laughed together again.

Missy's right eyebrow raised and she was just about to blurt out, "WHAT ON EARTH IS GOING ON HERE?!?!" when suddenly Mashela did the unthinkable.

"Paul," Mashela asked, "what do you think of Missy?"

Missy blinked noticeably.

*Well, **this** ought to be good.* Missy shut her mouth just before a sound came out.

Paul hesitated. "Nothing like suddenly changing the subject, Shea."

"Sorry," Mashela apologized. She flashed Missy a glance. "It's just that...I have to be honest with you because I know you'd be honest with me...Paul, I don't think she likes me."

"She's really a great girl," Paul said.

Missy smiled. *Take that, "Shea."*

"But don't you think she's kind of 'assuming' sometimes? I mean, the moment she saw me I think she assumed I was bad news. But you know me like few others do. You know I'm not bad."

"Well, that was quite a stunt you pulled on Alex last month," Paul pointed out. Missy was enjoying this. Mashela didn't know what she had coming when she started picking on Paul. Paul knew Mashela was different now that she was an NME agent. She had done some pretty terrible things and she wasn't sorry in the least. And now she didn't look like such "big stuff" in her little cage.

"No, Shea, I know you're not all bad," Paul countered. Missy didn't expect him to say that. Apparently, Mashela didn't either. For a moment, Missy saw her eyes look down in sadness. But she quickly snapped out of it. "And, yes, sometimes Missy can be assuming," he continued. "I'm kind of dealing with that right now."

Missy cocked her head. *Now what did he mean by—*

"Take this covenant brother/sister relationship we have," Paul explained. "She's just kind of assumed I wanted to be her covenant brother."

Missy felt her heart sink into her stomach. *Did he just say—*

"See, her father and my dad were best friends—covenant friends. The bond between them was inseparable. All they had they gave to each other. Even when my parents died, Mr. Ashton—that's Missy's dad—never stopped caring. When he found out recently that I was still alive, he took me in like his own. It was kind of awkward at first since I've been an orphan all my life, but I appreciate it. It means so much to me."

Mashela's eyes looked mysteriously hollow. But then, all of a sudden, she jumped back into the conversation and continued with her treachery. "But what about Missy?" she prompted.

"Well, after we discovered my dad and Missy's dad were covenant friends, Missy and I assumed that it made us like covenant brother and sister. And that was all great with me at first. But everything was so sudden. I think I may have acted on impulse instead of being wise. I'm just not sure if I'm ready for her to be my covenant sis—"

Missy let out a soft squeak as a warm tear dropped from the corner of her eye. Paul stopped mid-sentence and took a double-glance in her direction.

"Missy?!" Paul was obviously surprised to see her. His face drained of color.

"Shut up! Just shut up!" she cried, then immediately covered her mouth, realizing what she had just said. She stood still, not sure what to do next. She felt foolish standing where she wasn't supposed to be, now in the spotlight. Paul sat numb. Mashela wasn't looking in her direction. Was that...a smirk?

Missy tried again, softly this time. "I-I-I'm sorry." The lump in her throat was choking her words. She blinked to make the tears go away, but they rolled out instead. She looked at Paul again and gulped hard. She had to think. She had to get out of the shrinking room.

She ran to the door and slammed the open button. It hissed open and the guard couldn't move aside fast enough. Her feet tap-tap-tapped down the hall, making it sound like an army of soldiers was running with her. She'd made it to the lift when she heard the door to the holding room open again and another set of footsteps quickly coming her direction.

She pressed the open button and the lift doors slid aside. Missy got inside and hit the close button three times. They were shutting...they were shutting...they were shutting. They shut.

As she rode the lift down a level, she let out a soft sigh and rubbed away her tears. All she wanted to do was get back into bed, back into her dark room where no one could see her and she could cry herself to sleep. She could deal with this in the morning when she would most likely be furious and in a much better mood to deal with her "covenant brother."

The door opened.

Missy screamed—almost. Her mouth was covered by a protecting hand. Paul's. He was standing there in front of her, looking like a sad puppy. Huffing and puffing, he'd run all the way down the stairs to get to her before the lift stopped. But he was *not* on her list of favorite people right now. She locked her jaw. She wouldn't cry anymore.

"Get out of my way."

"You're not acting like a Superkid."

"Oh, and like you are."

"Not only that, but you're not acting like *Missy.*"

Missy put her hands on her hips. "Well, how am I supposed to act? Like I think Mashela is the most trustworthy person in the world? Like I didn't just hear what I heard? It doesn't take a Warren Technologies engineer to figure out what's going on here!"

Paul folded his arms across his chest. "Well, I'm not a Warren Technologies engineer, so maybe you can fill me in!"

Missy couldn't believe it. "Paul!" she cried. "You're sitting up at 10:30 *p.m.* talking about the good ol' times with someone who tried to kill not only Alex, but all of us! She admitted to Alex that when she shot at Rapper and Val's SuperCopter during this last vacation, she thought we were in there, too! If she could have killed us, she would have, Paul!"

"She didn't know that was us, Missy. She just thought it was some Superkids. If she had any idea I was on that 'copter, she wouldn't have shot it down."

"How do you know that?!"

"Because I know Shea!"

The hall fell silent. Paul put his hands on his hips. "But Missy, I'm not talking about her. I'm talking about you."

Missy looked down the hall. She was less than 100 feet from her room. "Well, I already know what you think about me." Before Paul could say another word, Missy darted to her room. He started after her, but she shut the door before he reached it. Inside, the room was dark.

Standing at the door, she could hear Paul approach and stand for a moment, deciding whether or not to knock. Missy let another tear out as she stood in silence. It slowly crawled down her cheek, taking the same path as her earlier tears. Shortly thereafter, Paul shuffled away, leaving their confrontation until morning.

▲   ▲   ▲

Missy let out a long, relaxing breath that sounded more like a huff. A thousand thoughts rushed through her mind as she removed her workout sweats and the blue scrunchie, and slid back into bed.

*Why had Paul said that? What was Mashela's agenda? Why didn't I just let well enough alone? Why didn't I just say what I was thinking? Why? Why? Why?*

Missy wiped away the tears that had dropped down and soaked her pillow. She didn't cry often, but when she did, she *did*. Her head pounded and her heart beat strong within her chest.

*Father God,* she prayed silently, *help me make sense of all this. I want to handle this like a Superkid, but I don't know what to do.*

Suddenly a response to her prayer came from across the room.

"I take it you didn't find what you expected," Valerie whispered in the darkness. The sound of her voice made Missy smile.

"You still awake?" Missy wondered, looking at the clock.

"You only left 10 minutes ago," Valerie pointed out. It was 10:45 p.m.

"How do I get into these messes?" Missy asked, staring at the ceiling.

"Mashela?" Valerie inquired.

"Paul," Missy answered.

"He was down there?"

Missy didn't respond, but her silence clued Valerie in.

Finally Missy said, "He said he didn't want me for a sister."

This time Valerie gave a long pause and then: "I'm sorry."

"You have any advice?" Missy wasn't ready to go to sleep yet. Valerie shifted in her bed.

"Just get your hand out of the cage, girl."

"What does that mean?"

"Ready for a late-night story?"

"Sure, anything."

"Well, when I was younger, my parents once told me about a time when they shared God's Word with a tribe that captured and killed monkeys."

"This is a pleasant story, Val."

"Now, I'm not finished yet. Let me finish," Valerie scolded playfully. "What was interesting was how they captured the monkeys. See, they'd set out a whole bunch of cages and then put a brightly painted stick inside each."

"So the monkeys would go inside the cages to get the stick and get caught, right?" Missy could just imagine it.

"Oh, no," Valerie said, "the monkeys were way too sharp for that. Instead, they'd just reach through the bars and grab the colorful stick."

"Smart monkeys."

"Not really. You see, the tribe members would make the sticks really large—too large to get out of the cage.

But the monkeys wanted the stick so bad they wouldn't let go. They would roll and kick and fuss and squeal, but they would *not* let go. And the natives would come along and bonk 'em on the heads."

"Stupid monkeys."

"That's why I say to get your hand out of the cage. I know you're smart enough to not enter into any old trap Satan sets. You're a Superkid and you know to stay out of sin."

Missy stayed silent.

"I'm just warning you as a friend," Valerie continued. "If Satan can't get you to get in his cage, he'll do the next best thing. He'll put something in there you might grab and not let go of."

"Like what?"

"The sin of offense. Mark 4:17 says that Satan will use little offenses to steal God's Word from our hearts. Getting offended or not getting offended is our choice. If the devil can get you to be offended at Paul and not forgive him, he'll have you trapped just as well as if you walked into the cage."

"And then he'll come and bonk me on the head?"

"You tell me."

"Sounds like that's exactly what he'd do. You're right, Val, as usual."

Valerie chuckled.

"I choose to forgive Paul now. I'll tell him when I see him next. I will not get my hand stuck in the cage! I will not be offen—"

Suddenly an alarm blasted throughout the Academy, causing both Missy and Valerie to jump out of bed. Three loud, short bursts were followed by the computerized message, "INTRUDER ALERT! INTRUDER ALERT! EMERGENCY LOCK-DOWN PROCEDURE INITIATED!"

Valerie tapped on the lamp, lighting up the room. She squinted at Missy. "Intruder alert? Someone's broken into the Academy?" she wondered.

"Either that," Missy responded, "or someone's broken out."

At once, the two girls received the obvious revelation. Together, they said the culprit's name.

"Mashela!"

Missy and Valerie darted out of their room, wearing their workout sweats and cross trainers. The alert sequences were still reverberating through the hallways. As their door hissed shut behind them, they nearly ran into the Blue Squad guys. Paul, Rapper and Alex were also in their workout suits.

"What's going on?" Rapper asked.

"Paul's best friend just broke out," Missy retorted, her mouth moving faster than her mind. Paul looked at her, obviously upset. She apologized.

"Are you sure?" Alex asked. His eyebrows were raised and his dark forehead wrinkled.

Valerie nodded. "I say we go down to her cell immediately and make sure. Because if she hasn't broken out, someone has broken in, most likely to get her."

"C'mon, let's go! We'd better check/The longer we wait, the farther she'll get!" Rapper rapped.

The Superkids ran down the hall, dodging an occasional cadet as they went. They all packed into the lift and zipped up a floor. The doors opened to a quiet hallway—too quiet.

All five members of the Blue Squad tumbled out of the lift and stopped in front of Commander Kellie. She was in similar-looking, gray workout sweats.

"Commander Kellie!" the group said in unison.

"Blue Squad," she acknowledged. "I just ran up here."

"Is it Mashela?" Paul asked. It was the first time Missy had heard him use her full first name.

"I imagine," the commander responded, nodding toward the holding room where Mashela resided. There was no guard. She tapped on her ComWatch. Commander Dana's face appeared on the watch-sized, video communication device. Commander Kellie often deferred to him for operations involving the main control room, his assigned area of command.

"Commander Dana—is Techno down there?" she asked. The commander affirmed that the robot was with him. "Have him meet us on Level 4, Holding Room 5," she continued.

"He's on his way," Commander Dana responded. "Out." The ComWatch went blank. With a top speed of 40 miles per hour, Missy knew Techno would join them soon.

Commander Kellie nodded and, together, the six ran down the hall. Missy found it hard to believe that only a half hour prior, she had been running down the hall in the opposite direction. They reached the door and Commander Kellie motioned for Paul, Missy and Alex to stand on the opposite side. She didn't want to leave a getaway option open. She pressed the door's button.

*Hisssssssss...*

The door opened, but no one ran out. Commander Kellie entered first, her arms positioned in front of her, ready for possible defense. Missy peeked in and saw Mashela lying on her cot, covered completely with a gray blanket.

Commander Kellie let down her defenses, realizing the room was empty except for Mashela on her cot. Making a mental note to track down whatever possible reason the guard had for abandoning his post, she walked toward the light blue force field. "Mashela?" she addressed. Mashela didn't move. Paul and Valerie joined the commander.

"Hey, Shea," Paul said with a nod, "Commander Kellie needs to talk to you." She didn't move. When Techno arrived, the remaining Superkids led him in.

"Why don't I hear her medband?" Valerie asked.

"Good question," said the commander beside her. Techno moved forward. Missy stayed at the door with Rapper and Alex. She didn't feel so good.

Commander Kellie moved to a small console on the wall, lifted up a cover and punched in a code on the numeric pad. The light blue force field vanished and Commander Kellie stepped forward into the chamber. Paul and Valerie joined her as general protection. The commander rolled Mashela over. Missy gasped. It wasn't Mashela! It was the guard. He had been knocked out.

"Techno!" the Blue Squad leader summoned. "Locate SKA 5-462-88-7 by her medband."

Techno wheeped and warbled. "Mashela Knavery is located on Level 4, in Holding Room 5," Techno reported, in his echoing electronic voice.

*"We're* on Level 4, in Holding Room 5," Paul argued with the robot.

"Her medband must be in this room somewhere," Valerie reasoned.

"Why can't we hear it?" Alex wondered.

*Beep...beep...beep...*

The Superkids froze. The soft beep echoed throughout the room. Each Superkid's eyes searched the air. Where was it coming from?

Missy looked up and screamed.

Mashela dropped down, landing squarely on her feet, directly in front of Missy and between Alex and Rapper. The door was behind her.

Missy gasped. "How did you—?"

"I muffled it, sister," Mashela quickly retorted. Instantaneously, she put her hand in Missy's face. Missy lunged back, but Mashela swept her foot in a half circle, tripping Missy and tossing her to the floor. Missy slammed down on her side, pinching her right arm beneath her.

Rapper came forward at Mashela, but she anticipated his move and kicked back, socking Rapper in his stomach. He keeled over, coughing.

"Techno!" Commander Kellie shouted, holding her Superkids back. The robot sped forward toward Mashela like a bowling ball toward pins. But Mashela jumped up, kicking off Techno like a diver off a springboard and sent the robot barreling into the wall. As she landed, she swept a small, pen-like device from her side and aimed it into Commander Kellie's eyes. A bright light flashed and the commander stepped back in shock, knocking into Paul and Valerie. Not missing a beat, Mashela flipped up the nearby switch cover and smacked the console. Before Commander Kellie, Paul and Valerie had an opportunity to flee the force field activated, trapping them inside.

"Thanks for putting in your password, Commander," Mashela taunted. "Makes things a bit easier for me."

"Shea, what are you doing?!" Paul shouted.

"Sorry, Paul. A girl's gotta do what a girl's gotta do."

Paul shook his head—disappointment written all over his face.

Mashela spun around and ran toward the door. Alex stood in the doorway, alone, blocking her way out. She stopped and looked at him. He looked at her. She lifted the small, pen device into the air.

"Don't flash that thing in *my* eyes," Alex said, stepping aside. "I've had enough bruises from you the last couple months."

Mashela pinched Alex's cheek. "You are sooo cute." She smiled with fiery eyes and ran out the door.

Alex ran forward and hit the deactivate button on the console. The force field vanished and Paul and Valerie ran out. Commander Kellie just stared forward.

"Is she gone?" Commander Kellie asked.

"You can't see?!" Valerie said, grabbing her arm.

"It's nothing. It'll wear off," Commander Kellie responded. "But you've got to get Mashela before she causes any real damage. Techno!"

The robot was spinning around, its optical modifiers inside its clear dome appearing a bit shaken up.

"Locate SKA 5-462-88-7 by her medband," the commander ordered again.

Techno beeped and bleeped. "Mashela Knavery is located on Level 4, heading down Corridor 14," Techno reported.

"Paul, Valerie, go!"

"Me, too!" Missy was on her feet. "I want to get this girl."

"Go!" the commander ordered. "Alex—I want you to stay here for technical help. Where's Rapper?"

Missy looked at her friend, still on the ground, holding his stomach. "I don't think Rapper's ready yet," she said.

"We'll pray for him," the commander said. "You guys *go!*" The three Superkids headed out the door with Paul in the lead.

"This way!" Paul shouted, turning right. They could hear Mashela's footsteps echoing in the hall.

"Boy, she *is* a covert-maneuvers specialist, isn't she?" Valerie added.

"She's just full of surprises," Missy replied. Paul shot Missy a glance. Missy shot back an I-told-you-so glare.

They rounded a corner and Missy spied a flash of Mashela's bright-orange clothing. "There!" she shouted, pointing. The Superkids sprinted.

"We can work this out!" Paul shouted ahead at Mashela.

"I'd rather do it on my terms!" she shouted back.

"I've *heard* about her terms," Valerie noted, breathing heavily from the run.

Mashela ran ahead out of sight. The Superkids kept after her. The echo in the hall made their footsteps sound like thunder.

"What a workout!" Valerie said between breaths. Missy's sweat suit was feeling heavy on her, too.

Suddenly the Superkids stopped. The hallway came to an intersection. They listened. They heard nothing.

Paul reached over to tap on his ComWatch, but realized he hadn't worn it. Neither Missy nor Valerie had theirs on either.

"We'll have to split up," Paul reasoned. "Val, you take the right corridor. Missy, you go down the left. I'll go straight." The girls readily agreed. After Commander Kellie, Paul was regularly put in charge.

Each Superkid quickly went their assigned way. Missy slowed down from her earlier run to a jog. She didn't want to run into an unwanted surprise. She made her way down the hallway, carefully listening for the beeping of the medband.

"Mashela?" Missy spoke as she made her way down the hall. "It didn't work. I know you were trying to separate me and Paul, but it didn't work. I won't be offended. Ha-ha!" Missy didn't feel much like laughing, but she knew what would get a response from the NME agent.

"There's nothing you can do to discredit Paul in my eyes!" she warned. "I'm going to talk to him and we'll work it out!"

The corridor remained silent.

Then she heard it.

*Beep...beep...beep.* At the end of the hall. At the next junction. She picked up her jog.

Then she saw it.

A long shadow, approaching, running, ready to cross the corridor Missy was in. Missy picked up her pace. This would be it. She would capture Mashela and sort everything out.

Missy drew closer to the corridor. The beeping was louder. The shadow was longer. She could hear heavy footsteps and the huffing and puffing of a long-distance runner. She was getting closer...closer...

The blond Superkid reached the juncture at the same moment the runner appeared. Missy screamed and shut her eyes tight. She leapt out with all she had and threw her full body weight at the trespasser.

*Wham!* The two collided and slammed onto the floor, skidding down the hall. They came to an awkward stop, but Missy had done it. She had really done it. She had captured Mashela.

*Beep...beep...beep...*

Wait a second...

That beeping wasn't coming from beneath her. It was coming from across the hall. She opened her eyes and they drew straight to the medband lying on the floor. Missy smiled. *I hit her so hard, I knocked her medband right off her!*

Missy pushed herself up and turned around to gloriously apprehend Mashela.

"Aaagh!" Missy shouted. It wasn't Mashela. It was *Paul.*

"Thanks, Missy," he said flatly, his face pressed into the crook of the wall and the floor. "I almost had her."

Missy let out a long, deep breath. Yep, she'd really done it.

"In summary," Commander Kellie concluded, "we have a dangerous NME agent somewhere in the Academy. She's been well trained and we should assume she knows as much about our procedures as we do. We have to find her, and *fast.* If she were to get out of the Academy and have record of our location...that could mean a *lot* of trouble." The commander's straight, brown hair rested upon her shoulders and accented her soft facial features. Her royal blue uniform was firmly pressed like the ones each of the Superkids wore. "Understood?" she asked.

The tired Superkids around the conference table nodded their heads. They had been up most of the night searching for Mashela to no avail. It was almost as though she had turned invisible. Techno couldn't locate her since she had taken off her medband and the huge Superkid Academy building had more nooks and crannies than the Superkids ever realized.

Now the Superkids were standing together at their frequently attended conference table, baffled. Because of the state of emergency, all training classes for the Blue Squad had been put on temporary hold.

Missy was glad when Commander Kellie's vision had returned at 4 a.m. She'd found out that the small, pen-like device Mashela had used to blind the commander was called a Hi-lighter. It was a harmless device, issued to the Academy's guards. Its effectiveness was immediate, but only temporary—just enough to gain the advantage when you needed to capture someone. Or, in Mashela's case, it was just enough to help her get away.

Missy felt awful. She felt partly responsible for her rival, like she had somehow provoked Mashela to start causing trouble. But inside her, she knew that wasn't the truth. Mashela had acted on her own, trying to stir things up from the start between Missy and Paul.

Missy looked over at Paul. Normally strong and adventure-driven, he looked rather worn with a big, black and blue bruise on the top of his forehead. She had replayed the tackle 100 times in her mind and kept asking herself why she hadn't taken one more second to ask the Holy Spirit for guidance. It would have made things a whole lot easier.

Paul looked over and caught Missy's eye. She looked down. She suddenly realized she still had never gotten around to telling Paul she forgave him for saying what he did. Surely he had his reasons...surely.

But part of her still didn't understand.

Just weeks ago they were in Nautical together—Missy's hometown—searching for clues to the whereabouts of Paul's parents. In just a three-day time span, they had grown closer than they'd ever been. And it wasn't a boyfriend/girlfriend type of thing. No, it was a rich, thick-as-blood, family type of thing. She stuck with him as his Christian sister, encouraging him as much as she could. She had really made an effort—and on that trip, there were *plenty* of opportunities for encouragement.

When they first arrived, Paul had found out the one clue he had—a blanket from his childhood—was given to nearly *every* child born in Nautical. Strike one. Then he'd found his stuffed bear at The Sawyer Orphanage— where he had grown up. It led him to a little shop back in Nautical...where the owner, a man named Fiffer, had lost his only record of the bear's owner in a murky bucket of cleaning water. Strike two. And then, the most disappointing strike of all: The paper files listing the name of Paul's mother were destroyed in a fire moments before Paul could get to them. Missy shuddered remembering the awful explosion and the look on Paul's face as his dreams of finding his parents were turned into ashes and rubble.

But then victory came. Paul discovered he had the same birthmark as a baby in a photo at Missy's house. That baby in the picture, of course, actually *was* Paul. The Ashtons, however, thought Paul had been killed in a tram wreck soon after the picture was taken...and on the very day Missy was born.

Paul's parents were on their way to the hospital to give their support to Mrs. Ashton since she was giving birth to Missy. Mr. Ashton and Missy's brother, Scott, had joined them. They were all coming together on a tram when it happened.

The tram skipped the track on a bridge and Paul's parents, Paul and Scott were thrown out of the tram and tossed into the river below. Mr. Ashton and Paul were the only ones who survived, though no one knew Paul had. In hindsight, all the pieces fit easily into place. Paul had been saved far down the river by a passerby and taken to an orphanage in a nearby town. He'd stayed there until age 10, when he came to Superkid Academy.

Missy would never forget the look on his face when Paul discovered it was *him* in that picture—Thomas Paul West. He was the son of Missy's dad's best friend. That was all Mr. Ashton had to hear. Immediately, he'd told Paul he was like one of the family. Paul had never felt like one of *anyone's* family. It was a moment Missy would never forget. It was also the moment when Missy felt like she had been given a gift—someone she could have as a brother, like Scott would have been. No, he wouldn't be a flesh-and-blood brother, but he would be a covenant brother. A covenant friend.

But things had changed since they'd come back to the Academy. Paul wasn't the same. The closeness they'd felt during their adventure together had waned. Paul sometimes seemed to distance himself from Missy, and she didn't know why. And then to have found out that every week since they'd returned, he had been spending time talking with an old friend from his orphanage made Missy unsure of how she should feel.

Especially when that old friend had taken up a career as an NME agent...a deceitful doer of no good whatsoever. Someone who had actually tried to kill Alex and Rapper and Valerie, and even Missy and Paul. Missy could feel her blood beginning to boil.

"Missy, are you paying attention to what I've been saying?" All eyes around the table were on Missy. She snapped out of her daydreaming.

"Huh? Oh...I'm sorry."

Commander Kellie smiled. "It's all right. I know everyone's tired. Alex just asked how she escaped. I explained that she apparently used her metal nameplate to nullify one portion of the force field and the sliding, metal door to nullify the opposite portion."

"Yeah," Alex said, "but what I can't figure out is how she got that metal door off there in the first place. She would have needed a small, but strong tool to unscrew it...or at least something that could work like one. And she didn't have anything like that."

Missy felt her stomach turn.

"Actually, that's not entirely true."

"Sure it is," Alex corrected her. "There are six flat screws around the inside of the door that she would have had to take out before she could have taken the door off."

"Right," Missy admitted. *"That's* true, but what's not entirely true is that she didn't have a small tool." All eyes were on Missy. She held up her right hand. "She stole my ring."

Paul's mouth dropped open. "You let her have your ring?! Missy, I gave that ring to you. That ring meant something."

"Did it?" Missy countered.

Commander Kellie didn't take her eyes off Missy. "Why didn't you report this?"

"I was going to," Missy said apologetically, "but..." Missy looked at Paul. "I got distracted."

Commander Kellie sighed her concern. "Well, we'll talk about *that* later. Right now we've got to find Miss Knavery."

▲　　▲　　▲

*"Ha-ha-ha-ha-ha-ha-ha!"*

*Missy felt her stomach turn at the laughter coming from around the hallway. It was unmistakable. It was Mashela's. Missy wanted to turn. She wanted to run away...but she couldn't. She felt compelled to go to her...compelled to see her.*

*Missy rounded the corner and found herself on a long set of twisting, metal stairs reaching upward... upward...upward. She looked up and saw Mashela's feet taking the steps two-by-two. If she reached the sky, she would get away. Missy couldn't allow that. She ran up the steps after her, each step sounding like a clanging cymbal. She had to reach her.*

*Step after step she ran...but she wasn't getting any closer. She was exhausting herself, but she had hardly moved at all.*

*Mashela was almost there! She was going to reach the sky! Missy couldn't let her reach the sky! No!*

*With everything within her, Missy shot forward like a rocket and caught the sinner's hand. She could feel the ring on Mashela's finger slice into her own skin as she grabbed her. Missy was going to stop her. She wasn't going to get away. Missy caught a thick lock of Mashela's hair with her other hand and pulled.*

*The painful action caused Mashela to stop in her tracks. Missy plowed into her and was knocked to the ground. Mashela stood solid as a brick wall. Missy looked up.*

*Mashela flipped her head around and looked at Missy. Missy gasped. Mashela's eyes weren't the hard brown Missy had remembered. They were stone blue. They were Missy's eyes...*

With a start, Missy woke up. Her heart was beating like a startled bird in sudden flight. As her eyes focused, she realized she was sitting outside at the table the Superkids normally occupy for meals. A cool breeze brushed over her skin, sending a chill up her spine.

Her four friends from the Blue Squad were setting down their trays on the table in front of her. Alex had a second tray he placed in front of Missy.

"You all right?" he asked as he slid the bacon and eggs past Missy's nose.

"Uh, yeah...yeah," she responded. "I think I fell asleep."

"I'm not surprised," Valerie punctuated. "You didn't get any beauty sleep last night."

"Not that that makes you any less beautiful," Rapper said, smiling wide.

Missy shot him a playful smile, shaking off the dream. "Ha-ha. You couldn't sound any more sincere, could you?"

The group laughed.

"Would you believe I just dreamed about Mashela?" Missy asked everyone.

"She really is giving you trouble, huh?" Paul asked. Missy nonchalantly shoved a forkful of scrambled eggs into her mouth. "No, not at all," she responded with her mouth full. If he was going to act as though nothing had happened between them, she would, too.

Paul stuffed half of a piece of toast into his mouth. "Aw ewe suw?" he mumbled through the bread.

Missy shoved another bite of eggs into her mouth. "Eth, I'n suw!"

Valerie started waving her hands. "You guys are grossing me out!"

Paul and Missy began to laugh. Somehow, the moment had turned into a non-confrontational way to say, "I'm sorry." Missy enjoyed hearing Paul laugh with her—it had been a while.

Rapper shoved a sausage link into his mouth. "Aaah, ewe gyth aw grothine me ow thoo." He began to laugh. Paul and Missy laughed harder. Alex was already holding his side and couldn't even manage to get any food in his mouth, let alone say anything silly.

Valerie folded her arms across her chest. "You guys, that is *so gross!* Do you know how gross that is?"

Everyone kept laughing.

"Not to mention dangerous," she continued. "I don't want to have to practice the Heimlich maneuver on any of you."

By now, everyone had tears rolling down their faces.

"You guys have had way too little sleep," Valerie scolded. She put her hand over her eyes. "This is so embarrassing. Here sits the Blue Squad at breakfast, a shining example to all other squads and cadets, losing it big-time."

Missy wasn't about to let Valerie out of the group laugh, though. With food still puckered in her cheeks, she tapped Valerie on the shoulder.

Valerie looked sternly at Missy. "What?" she asked.

Missy held up her skinned thumb.

"Ith been woundeth!" she cried.

Valerie tried her hardest, but she couldn't keep a straight face, which made it all the funnier.

Missy looked around the table at her laughing friends. Silently, she thanked God for them.

▲   ▲   ▲

After breakfast, when the Blue Squad reported back to the main control room on Level 2, Commander Kellie had some disturbing news.

"But first the good news," Commander Kellie said. She held up the small, pen-like device Mashela had used earlier. "We found *this* right in here this morning."

"The Hi-lighter," Rapper said.

"And my eyes aren't going to get hit with it again," Commander Kellie said with a smile. "It goes into safekeeping." She put the Hi-lighter into her uniform pant pocket.

"Wait a second," Paul said. "What was she doing on Level 2?"

"Now for the bad news..." Missy said under her breath.

"Superkids," Commander Kellie said, "it has suddenly become more imperative than ever to track down Mashela Knavery."

The Superkids exchanged wondering glances.

"We've discovered that Mashela made a late-night phone call," she explained, "but it was too short to trace."

Techno rolled closer. His boxy, snow-white frame glistened under the control room's lights. He let out a series of beeps.

"But after that," the robot reported, "we discovered a low-key, long-distance homing signal emanating from within the bandwidth of probable communications."

"What does that mean?" Missy wondered aloud.

Alex interpreted. "It means Mashela's calling for help." Alex placed a dark hand on Techno's dome. Techno warbled.

"That's exactly it," Commander Kellie agreed with a nod.

"Yeah," Alex said after a pause, "and since we've discovered it's within our communications bandwidth, we realized we should be able to decipher it using our standard set of algorithms."

Missy had no idea what Alex said, but that was nothing new. A good friend and integral part of the Blue Squad, Alex seemed to understand things about mathematics and computers that the rest of them had yet to grasp. This strength made Alex stand out as the technical leader of the bunch. When Alex, the youngest, first attended Superkid Academy, he'd felt inferior to the rest. But the anointing of God and the spirit-strengthening faith exercises of the Academy had brought Alex a long way...not to mention the few times he'd had to deal with personal run-ins with NME. He certainly had grown a lot. Thank God for Alex.

"I think I get it," Valerie said enthusiastically.

"You do?" Missy had to ask. Valerie looked back as if to ask, *What's so odd about that? Don't you get it?* Missy shrugged her shoulders.

"All Alex is saying," Commander Kellie explained, "is that if we found Mashela's message, we should be able to read it. And we did."

The eyes of all the cadets were on their faithful commander.

"What we found out," she revealed, "is that Mashela is sending out a standard homing subsignal at 27.225 megahertz."

"How primitive," Alex observed.

"Indeed," the commander agreed. "Primitive enough for us to overlook. And if Techno hadn't been jostled last night, he wouldn't have had to link up with our mainframe for diagnostics and we may never have known."

"So what good is her signal?" Valerie questioned. Missy just listened.

"Good enough to summon a preset Serfsled."

Missy had heard of a Serfsled before. It was a small, airborne sled, usually used as a high-tech "lifeboat" of sorts for large vessels. Because of this, it could be controlled remotely or even summoned to find you should you send for it with a homing signal. It was a fast, silent and especially maneuverable two-person vehicle.

"You think it's a Serfsled from an NME ship?" Paul questioned.

Commander Kellie shook her head. "No, I don't. Mashela lost face with NME when she failed her last mission and wound up in our holding area. She risks too much going back there right away."

"Not to mention that she has too much pride," Missy interjected. Commander Kellie nodded.

"Plus," she continued, "the homing signal was sent out at exactly 27.225 megahertz—that's not a common NME frequency. I think she's made a deal to use someone else's Serfsled."

"Whose?" Paul asked.

Rapper, who had been quiet until now, sighed. "She's gone underground and made a deal with the Vipers."

"It's their frequency," Commander Kellie agreed.

Rapper had reason to be upset. He knew the Vipers all too well. He used to be one. The Vipers were one of the many under-city gangs that lived by their own set of rules. They didn't follow the Superkids or NME. They had their own way of doing things. So it wasn't surprising that Mashela would contact them for help. What was surprising was that they would help her.

Missy had to ask the question forming in her mind. "So Mashela contacted the Vipers and they've programmed one of their Serfsleds to follow the homing signal and come get her. But what do they get out of it?"

"Maybe something, maybe nothing, for now," Rapper said. "I was a member of the Vipers for four years. I know. They may be willing to help her out just so she'll owe them one in the future—in case they ever need it."

"And Mashela *has* the resources," Commander Kellie interjected.

"Working with an under-city gang doesn't sound like Mashela's style," Paul noted. "She's always teamed up with the big guns, like NME."

"But she's desperate," Alex added. "She's lost face with NME and is trapped in Superkid Academy."

Commander Kellie added, "I wouldn't underestimate her."

To cover the base thoroughly and efficiently, the Blue Squad split up. Alex and Techno were put in charge of keeping constant track of the area surrounding Superkid Academy. If that beacon reached its source, a Serfsled was on its way—and they had to stop it before it arrived.

Rapper and Valerie were teamed up as one search party and Paul and Missy were teamed up as the other. Missy could see God's hand in this—she had been wanting to talk to Paul alone all morning, to officially apologize, and until now she hadn't had the opportunity.

Of course, throughout the rest of the Academy, cadets and Superkids from other squads were on alert. Daily activities had to continue, but they were ordered to keep special watch, as well as keep sensitive areas secure. They didn't want Mashela to show up some-place where she could jeopardize critical information.

After praying together for help and protection, the two groups were off. Missy and Paul decided to start in the corridor they had last seen Mashela in and work their way forward and up. Rapper and Valerie, on the other hand, started in the same place, but worked their way backward and down. It could take them several hours, but they were determined to find her.

Once Missy and Paul were alone, she couldn't hold it in any longer. They were walking down a corridor looking for any evidence of clues, tampering with vent covers or other suspicious activity. The familiar, round ceiling lights were buzzing softly, spreading light along the gray hallway.

Missy stopped in her tracks. After a couple steps alone, Paul turned around.

"What?"

"What what?" Missy answered.

"Why are you stopping?"

"I have something I have to tell you, Paul." Missy was looking at the ground. Paul stood straight and waited. Missy raised her eyes to meet his. "I...I'm sorry."

Paul shook his head. "No, Missy, wait. I'm the one who's sorry. I never should have said what I did."

"But I'm sorry, too," Missy apologized again. "I got offended at you and I shouldn't have. I don't want my hand in a cage like some stupid monkey."

"What?"

"I'm just saying...I realized that my responsibility is only to make sure I care about you as a sister should. It's not my responsibility to make sure you care about me. Does that make any sense? Anyway, that's all." There. She did it. She said it all.

"Thanks, Missy," Paul whispered. He shuffled his feet. "Everything has happened so quickly, you know? One day I'm an orphan, alone in the world, without a family. Then *wham!* the next day your parents were willing to take me in as their own...and you were willing to be my covenant sister. It's a lot all at once."

Missy was looking down again. It was too hard to look directly into Paul's brown eyes for her next question, but it welled up within her. She swallowed hard.

"Can you just tell me one thing?"

Paul sounded wary. "...All right..."

"Why do you like Mashela more than me?"

"Missy, I—"

Missy stomped her foot. "Let me finish!" she pouted. The words came out stronger than she wanted. Paul put up his hands, surrendering.

"I know you knew her before me," she began, "but she doesn't even know Jesus. I'm sure she was like a sister when you knew her, but your life has changed. *Her* life has changed. Paul, I want to be the one who's like a sister to you. I can take it—what is it about her that you like better?"

Paul's tone of voice was defensive. "Missy, I don't like her better. I—"

"You've spent more time with her these past few weeks than you have with me!" Missy whirled around, upset. She wanted to know the answer.

"You're right," Paul admitted. "I have." Missy wasn't sure how to respond. She didn't expect him to agree with her. "But you have to understand," he continued, "I haven't seen Shea in nearly five years, and back then she was the closest thing I had to a sister. I can't just pretend that's not true. Seeing her after all these years...well, sure, I wanted to catch up with her and talk about old times a bit, but believe it or not, I've been witnessing to her."

Missy turned around. "You have not." She didn't believe it.

"I promise," he responded, lifting his left hand and covering his heart with his other. "You're right—I've changed a lot. And I just want to share that with her. For nearly five solid weeks, I've been witnessing to her after my daily duties are done, but she doesn't seem to hear a word I say. She's been through so much...and made so many bad decisions."

Missy's forehead wrinkled. "Really?"

Paul looked up at one of the buzzing lights and then back at Missy.

"Shea's had a tough life. And that, combined with the decisions she's made, have made her who she is. I know if she repented before God, He would turn her life around, but her heart is hard. I've been praying for her for years. I guess I thought maybe this was an answer to that prayer. But the more I talk to her, I realize it may not be right now. I think God is using this time for me to plant seeds of His Word in her heart, seeds that will grow...then maybe sometime when we all least expect it, she'll give her life to Him."

"I tried to pray for her last night," Missy said, "but when I started, I just thought of all the rotten things she's done. It was hard for me to focus."

Paul nodded. "Shea said when she was young, she was taken from her parents. She says it was because they didn't love her or something. I don't know if that's true, but I do know she was put into the custody of another couple that must have cared even less for her. For a couple years, the man beat her, he hurt her...I can't imagine."

"I had no idea," Missy said, mouth gaping. "What about the man's wife?"

"She didn't ever tell the police and she belittled Shea constantly. The state finally found out about it and took her from them and placed her in the orphanage where we met. Oh, and would you believe neither one *ever* told Shea that they loved her? For the first seven years of her life, Shea never *ever* heard the words, 'I love you.'"

Missy couldn't believe it. "She lived seven years before ever hearing the words, 'I love you'?"

Paul nodded. "And I doubt she's heard them much since joining NME."

Missy bit her lip.

"That still doesn't give her an excuse for acting the way she does—deceiving and hurting others."

"No, it doesn't. But it does show us where she's coming from."

"I don't like her."

Paul was taken aback. "Missy, what's gotten into you? I've known you for four years, and suddenly you're not your usual, kind and caring self."

Missy was silent for a moment and then she softly asked, "You think I'm kind and caring?"

"Do I think—? Yes!! Missy, when I got the lame idea to go on a quest all by myself—when I didn't think I needed any help—who insisted on coming along?"

Missy didn't answer.

"Who stowed away in my luggage and made me stay at her parents' house?"

"Me," she said with a shy smile, looking up.

"That's right. Missy, have you ever stopped to consider what would have happened if you hadn't cared—and if you had gone to Calypso Island with Rapper and Val instead?"

"Well, Val may not have gotten lost."

"Yeah, or maybe you *both* would have gotten lost. That's not the point. The point is that I never would have stayed at your house. I never would have met your parents. And we never would have found out—*together*—who my parents were." Paul punched the word "together."

Missy thought for a moment and then looked into Paul's eyes.

"But that's just it," she admitted. "We had this great adventure together and discovered who your parents were—and who you are. Finding out our families were so close showed me that I may suddenly have someone in my life who can be like my big brother, Scott, would have been. I never even got to know him. That's why I want to get to know you as a covenant brother. Not just a friend—a *brother*. And lately you've been spending more time talking with the enemy than you have with me."

Paul looked around the corridor. "Well, I don't know how to be close to someone like a brother," he said. "I've been an orphan all my life. You heard us talking in there. I grew up independent and a troublemaker. I'm learning, but I can't just be the perfect covenant brother overnight."

"Paul," Missy said softly, "I don't expect you to be perfect. All I want is for you to work as hard at being my covenant brother as you're working at remembering old times with Mashela. She's just feeding your old life, Paul. You have a new identity—in Christ. Together, we'll become stronger as we guide each other into His ways. We can build each other up in the Word."

"I'm solid with my covenant in God. It's just...I don't know if I'm ready to commit to being in a *brother/ sister* covenant."

"So what—you gave me that ring on impulse?"

"Well...does it matter? It's lost now anyway."

"I can't believe you just said that. So it's my fault that our friendship isn't working?"

"Our friendship's working fine—it's this covenant thing between us that's not working for me."

"What?! Covenant *thing?* Oh, that's—"

"Guys!" It was the ComWatches. Paul and Missy looked at each of their ComWatches and saw Rapper's serious face.

"What's up?" Paul asked all business-like. Missy huffed. For now, this would have to be put abruptly on hold.

"It's Mashela," Rapper replied. "I think Val and I have found her. Meet us in the back area of Sub-Level 3 immediately."

Finally, some progress. Missy spoke into her ComWatch. "We're on our way."

Sub-Level 3 was a dark, rarely used series of corridors located halfway between Level 2 (containing the Main Control Room) and Level 3 (hosting the Superkids' living quarters). The hallways were about 6 feet wide with a series of tracks extending down most. The tracks were used for fast transport from one area of the sub-level to another. The cars that rolled along the tracks were dirty, gray vehicles that looked like open boxes with a series of gears on the front. A single, round, white light lit their predetermined path. Superkid Academy used the series of boxcars only when repairs had to be made within the Academy's electronic or mechanical systems. The tunnel gave them easy access to these networks. When Paul and Missy arrived, they realized it was the perfect hideout for Mashela Knavery...and the perfect place to secretly send out a beacon to the world.

"Well, here we all are," announced Rapper. "This place is so dark and damp—it reminds me of the Vipers' hideout I used to live in." Rapper shivered—shaking off the thoughts of his past life. "No good memories here."

"So what did you find?" Paul wondered.

Valerie held out her hand. A small, fluorescent-orange thread lay in it, like a neon scribble across her palm.

"That's from Shea's Academy-issued uniform," Paul realized.

"Bingo," emphasized Rapper.

Missy looked around, searching for other clues, but didn't see any. "There are so many nooks and crannies in this place," she observed, "I don't know how we're ever going to find her."

Valerie, standing between Missy and Rapper, grabbed each of their hands. "I know how," she said emphatically. "We'll pray."

Valerie, who wanted to one day be a commander in the Academy herself, was bold and confident before the group. Paul filled in the missing link in the circle of prayer and Valerie began to pray.

"Father God, we come before You in the Name of Jesus. We know You love Mashela Knavery and, for her sake, we're wanting to find her today. We pray You would lead us directly to her. Lord, we pray for the wisdom You said You'd give us when we ask. Help us to be sensitive to Your Spirit and put aside any personal issues—we do not have a spirit of fear, but of power and love and self-control! Thank You, Father God. We agree today in Jesus' Name and, according to Matthew 18:20, we know You are here with us. Amen!"

"Amen!" repeated the other Superkids in unison.

"All right," Paul instructed, his right hand waving through the musty air, "let's all split up and sweep this place as fast as we can."

The Superkids nodded.

"And if you find her, communicate through your ComWatch immediately. Remember, Shea is highly trained—we need to work together to beat her at her game."

The Superkids dispersed and Missy moved forward, choosing the nearest corridor to begin her search.

The hallway was a dark-steel color, forbidding and entirely enclosed. The hollow sounds of each of her friends' footsteps faded behind her as she walked deeper through the sub-level. Periodically, Missy stopped to listen for sounds up ahead: the shuffling of feet, the near-silence of nervous breathing, the clicking of stolen electronics.

A sudden feeling of being alone brushed over Missy like a midwinter chill. As she approached the first juncture in her walk, it hit her that Mashela Knavery, mean-spirited agent extraordinaire, could be waiting around the corner to pounce. Missy slowed her steps, hoping that the next approaching juncture and each one after it would be completely empty.

Missy stopped and closed her eyes for a brief moment. She wouldn't allow fear to grab hold of her. Not her.

"For God has not given me a spirit of fear," she whispered, quoting 2 Timothy 1:7 as Valerie had. "He gave us a spirit of...of..." A picture of Mashela formed in her mind. She was laughing behind the light blue force field in the holding room. Missy thought of Paul sitting there, talking to her, laughing with her. It angered Missy.

And didn't she have the right to be mad? Didn't she have full right to get upset? It would almost seem wrong *not* to strike out against that deceiver.

Missy opened her eyes. Her blood was boiling. But the fear still seemed to wrap around her. She began to speak out another verse—this time from Psalm 91—as she stepped forward.

"I will say to the Lord, 'You are my place of safety and—'" Suddenly another flash of Mashela appeared in her mind. This time, it was her hand coming open-palmed into Missy's face. She saw the girl sweep her foot in a half circle and cause Missy to slam down on her side. Missy touched her arm. She could almost feel the pain again, surging through it as when it had been pinned down by her own weight.

Missy tucked a thread of blond hair behind her right ear as she attempted to finish quoting the Bible verse she had begun a moment ago...but she couldn't even remember which verse she had begun.

The dim light bulbs in the hall cast eerie shadows across the upcoming intersection. Missy gulped. Then she heard it.

*Click-click-click.*

Footsteps.

The sound, though virtually inaudible, seemed to echo in the chamber. Missy began breathing heavier. Her forehead began to perspire in a cold sweat. She pressed against the closest wall and scooted down to the intersection. She worked hard to stay as quiet as a mouse sneaking a chunk of cheese in front of a sleeping cat.

She moved closer...closer...

Closer...

An elongated shadow stretched into the open area.

Missy could almost hear the cautious, soft breathing of her enemy...or was that herself?

Missy drew closer, inching along the wall.

Suddenly the enemy around the corner froze. She couldn't have been more than 10 feet away. Missy could hear her shuffle. Missy was breathing nervously. She knew Mashela was onto her.

She stood frozen. One of them would have the element of surprise. One of them would jump out in front of the other. Who would have the advantage—she or Mashela?

"Missy!"

Missy's eyes grew wide and her heart thumped as she heard her name shout out from her ComWatch. She brought it up and saw Valerie's face. She slapped the watch off. Her cover was blown.

A split second later, from around the corner, her enemy jumped. Her feet landed hard, sending a thumping echo through the corridor. Missy screamed at the surprise and cowered back, not having time to think.

"Missy!"

It was Valerie's voice again. Missy stared down at her ComWatch. Yes—if she could let Valerie see Mashela's face, Valerie would know something was wrong. But the screen on the ComWatch was blank.

"Missy!"

The voice wasn't coming from the ComWatch...

Missy looked up in fright and her mouth dropped in surprise. It wasn't Mashela standing there—it was Valerie!

"Missy, what's wrong?" Valerie wondered aloud, reaching forward to help. Her dark brown eyebrows were high, wrinkling her forehead in concern.

Missy was still shaking, but managed to pull herself together and push herself back up. An embarrassing remembrance of her rushing into Paul earlier passed through her mind.

"I-I'm sorry," she said. "You just gave me quite a start. I thought you were Mashela."

Valerie searched Missy's eyes, piercing into her soul. "Missy, remember 2 Timothy 1:7—God did not give us a spirit that makes us afraid. He gave us a spirit of power and love and self-control."

"I know that verse!" Missy stated defensively.

Valerie paused. "I...didn't say you didn't...I was just wanting to remind you—"

"All right, all right," Missy stammered. "I know." Missy pulled her hand down over her face, smoothing out the stressful tightening caused by fear.

Valerie placed her right hand softly on Missy's left shoulder—Missy knew it must have felt tense—and she looked Missy squarely in the eyes.

"Friend," Valerie addressed her, "are you sure your hand is out of the cage? You need to be able to think clearly and be spiritually alert right now. If you're not, you need to leave it to the rest of us."

Missy nodded and smiled. "Thanks, Val." She let out a long, relaxing breath. "Yeah, I'm OK. Paul and I have been ironing things out. I guess I'm still just a little on edge, but I'll be all right."

Valerie let go and stepped back. She smiled sweetly and pointed upward. "God is faithful. We can trust Him every step of the way."

Missy nodded again. Valerie was right. She just had to rely on the Lord and His anointing power to help her.

Missy's 11-year-old roommate began to continue her search when suddenly her ComWatch came alive. Missy turned her own wristband communicator back on and saw Rapper. His eyes were wide.

"Guys! I found her! No...wait...I think she's found me! I'm at coordinates—uph!" The screen twirled in all directions as the ComWatch on Rapper's wrist caught the scene. Rapper appeared to be knocked down. Then a pair of hard, brown eyes appeared on the view screen and it went black.

"Rapper!" Valerie shouted, rolling her finger over the fine-tuning knob on her ComWatch. But it was no use. There was no response.

Paul's face abruptly appeared on each of their ComWatches.

"You guys receive that?" he wondered.

"Yeah," Missy responded. She felt numb. Mashela had just whittled them down by one.

"Father, we thank You that Psalm 91:15 confirms that You are with us in trouble," Valerie confessed. "We believe that You will protect Rapper."

"I agree," Paul said. "Now listen. Be extra cautious and let's find that girl. She doesn't realize what she's doing. Out."

Missy disagreed. Mashela knew *exactly* what she was doing.

Valerie waved without much thought to the action and took off jogging down the hallway in the direction she had been heading. Missy heard her praying in the spirit under her breath as she left. Missy continued her own stride forward. She gritted her teeth and folded her hands into fists. The action made her feel more in control, though her mind contradicted those feelings.

As she walked, Missy began praying in the spirit also, speaking out words the Holy Spirit stirred up within her. But as Missy continued, her thoughts once again turned to Mashela. She could almost see the NME agent's eyes again, staring out from the ComWatch. She could see her knocking Rapper down—before he even knew what was coming.

"Stop it!" Missy said aloud, startling herself. She stopped and looked around. Why couldn't she stop thinking about Mashela? What kind of hold did this girl have on her? *God,* she prayed silently, *I pray for insight.* She continued walking.

Missy walked and jogged from one turn to another, always being cautious...and a bit apprehensive. She couldn't figure out exactly why she was feeling that way. Usually, her attitude was to "go for it!" "Charge into the challenge!" "Run for the prize!" But she was feeling worn today, like a long-distance runner in the last stretch of a race.

The more she thought about it, the more she realized it wasn't like her. She remembered when she was in the second grade and she came home with her first bad grade on a report card. Most kids would have been ashamed. Most kids would have felt defeated. But not Missy. Missy Crystal Ashton was no quitter. She could remember it as if it were yesterday. She came home, walked over to the big, leather chair her father was reclining in and presented him with her report card...and the following words: "Daddy, here's my report card. You'll notice that my grade in English is not a happy grade. But don't worry. The next time you get a report card from me, English will be my *best* grade." How could a father get upset about that?

Sure enough, time told the true tale—and on her next report card, Miss Ashton had a shining grade in English. That's the way Missy handled trouble. She beat it. She stood up against it fearlessly and beat it.

*Sfffft!*

Missy froze and felt a surge of adrenaline rush from her head and plummet into the pit of her stomach. The tearing sound came from around the next corner.

*Sffft!*

There it was again. Missy pressed herself up against the wall and inched down to the corner. First things first: she turned off her ComWatch. She didn't need it blowing her cover again. Next, Missy grabbed her hair and pulled it back out of the way. Then, slowly... cautiously...she stole a glance around the corner.

It was really Mashela this time. For a second, Missy wondered why she was the one blessed to find her. She breathed hard and cooled down. The rival wasn't coming her way. She was standing still. Missy glanced again. She had Rapper with her—and he was very obviously there against his will.

Sitting on the ground, he had thick, silver duct tape across his mouth and around his wrists. It was the ripping of tape she had heard. Rapper's legs were free, but he wasn't running anywhere because she also had him blindfolded. Missy couldn't figure out what on earth she was doing.

She wasn't asking him questions and she wasn't hurting him. She just had him bound. Missy glanced back a third time—ever so cautious. Mashela was standing about halfway down the corridor, off the side of the tracks. A fire exit was behind her.

*That's it!* Missy reasoned when she saw Mashela begin to tamper with the electronic controls at the side of the door. *She's heading out...and no doubt she plans to go up—straight up—to the Level 5 Superkid Mission Deployment Ramp.* It was on the top of the building and it was the perfect place to meet a Serfsled.

Missy turned her ComWatch volume down as low as she could.

"Guys!" she whispered after setting it to send out an alert to the entire Blue Squad. "I found her!"

"She's got Rapper here," Missy reported to the crew. "She has him all tied up, but I don't know what she plans to do with him."

On the screen, Missy saw Valerie's eyes close. "She's probably hoping to use him as insurance for her escape."

Paul's face appeared on screen. "Where are you, Missy?"

Missy's lip twisted. "I don't know."

"You don't know?!"

"Hey!" she said in a hushed whisper. "This place is like a maze! And I guess I got to thinking about other things..."

Paul's head turned down to look at her as if to say, *Girl, how could you possibly be thinking about other things?!* Missy wondered *that* herself.

"Well, there's a fire door here," she reported.

Alex's face: "There are 16 fire doors on Sub-Level 3, Missy."

"Listen," she said forcefully, but still whispering, "I think she's planning to take the fire escape stairs straight up to the Level 5 Deployment Ramp—she could catch a Serfsled from there. It's wide open."

Commander Kellie's face appeared next. "Good thinking, Missy. That makes sense. And Alex has detected a small vehicle coming straight for Superkid Academy. OK, Superkids, here's the plan. I want everyone up to the deployment ramp. Missy, you keep an eye on Mashela and make sure she doesn't go somewhere else. First priority is rescuing Rapper. *Then* we'll go after Mash—"

*Ka-BOOOOOOOMMMMMM!!!*

The Academy reverberated with the shock of an explosion. Missy wanted to scream, but stifled even a peep. She looked around the corner at Mashela and saw her smiling.

"What'd she do?!" Missy whispered into the ComWatch.

Alex shouted, "Oh, great! She disabled the main power grid! We're losing power throughout the Academy!"

Suddenly the lights in the dark tunnels flickered and then blacked out. Mashela let out a high-pitched laugh.

"She is really off her rocker," Missy whispered to herself.

"I heard that."

Missy's eyes grew wide as Mashela's face filled the screen. She was wearing Rapper's ComWatch.

"My orders still stand," Commander Kellie assured them. "Superkids, I want no more communication on these ComWatches. Out!" The ComWatch went blank.

*Bam!* Around the corner, Mashela kicked the fire door and it willingly gave way. She dragged Rapper to his feet, pushed him out in front of her and left the building. Missy charged after her, placing herself right behind the door before it shut. She held it open by a centimeter. Her rival was on the other side…and she knew Missy was near.

*Here we go!* she thought as she slowly pressed the heavy door open.

A shaft of light pierced through the crack around the door, illuminating the darkened hallway. Missy knew she couldn't stay put—she had to keep an eye on Mashela. And if she could, she had to help Rapper.

Carefully listening, Missy could hear Mashela step up the fire escape. As Missy had surmised, she was making her way to the Superkid Deployment Platform on the wide roof of the Academy, three tall stories straight up from where Missy now stood.

The steady *clang, clang, clang* of feet against the iron stairway told Missy that Mashela and Rapper weren't moving fast. No doubt, Rapper's blindfold complicated matters. What did it matter to Mashela? As far as she knew, she had just left her only opponents in the dark.

Missy desired to stay hidden, but she knew in order to keep an eye on her rival, she had to step out onto the fire escape. Softly, she did. The crisp, outside air hit her skin and she winced. The late-morning sun was hiding behind clouds. She looked straight up and, through the steelwork, she could see Mashela climbing the stairs of the fire escape behind Rapper. She was pushing him along, prodding him like a farmer prods a herd of cattle.

Mashela Knavery's long, black hair stood out against the neon-orange outfit she still wore. The soles of her shoes were off-white and each step was deliberate. A chill crawled down Missy's spine as she had the eerie feeling she had been in this situation—or at least seen it—once before.

*BAM!*

Missy whirled around as the fire door shut with a boom. The thundering sound reverberated in her ears like a gunshot in the mountains. Missy looked up through the fire escape—and saw Mashela looking down at her, angry at the intrusion to her perfect plan.

Hearing the door slam, Rapper stopped moving. He was twisting his head, surely wondering what was going on around him—let alone where he was. Mashela pushed him.

"Keep going!" she shouted. She looked up two and a half stories to the top of the building, then she gazed back down at Missy. The young Superkid whirled around toward the door again, hoping for protection. She reached down for the doorknob...but it wasn't there. The door's surface was smooth from top to bottom, a safeguard against intruders.

"Oh God, oh God, oh God, oh God, oh God," Missy pleaded as fear surrounded her. She couldn't figure out where it had come from. Where was the clearheaded, don't-make-a-big-deal-about-the-problem person she usually was? Contrary to her nature, Missy just wanted to *get away.*

The NME agent above saw the fear written all over Missy's face. She seized the opportunity. She started running down the steps two by two. Missy banged against the door twice, shouting, but she knew there was no one on the other side to open it. She realized she had only a few seconds to make a clear choice—face her enemy or retreat. Though it was against everything within her, Missy chose the latter.

She was a little over two stories up and there were stairs still leading down. Missy grabbed the railing for support and started bounding down the metal stairs. But Mashela was fast. Missy hadn't even leapt down half a flight when Mashela grabbed Missy's royal blue Superkid uniform and yanked. Missy was caught off balance and knocked backward into Mashela, who was still coming forward. Missy struggled to get away, but Mashela had her in her grasp.

Missy's long hair got in her own face and she couldn't see what was happening. She screamed. Mashela was breathing heavily from her run, but otherwise she was unexpectedly collected. Missy worked to regain her composure. She knew she couldn't beat Mashela without it.

Missy pushed herself up and pulled Mashela with her. Mashela lost her balance, fell forward and hit the railing at the next base of the stairs. She grabbed the railing and, to avoid a bad hit, she flipped over the top. Her body came straight down and dangled in the air. Her feet were reaching for solid ground—but it was nearly 50 feet down.

The Superkid moved over to her, feeling spent. Mashela's knuckles were turning white from hanging. Missy looked down at her. She put her hands on her hips.

"You're not such hot stuff now are you?" she said between breaths.

"You think this is over?"

"You think it's not?"

Mashela smiled...but not a sweet, picture-perfect smile. It was one of those smiles that says, *"I know something you don't."*

Missy's eyebrows dove in toward her nose as she watched Mashela pull her feet up beneath her and swing back. Before Missy realized what was happening, Mashela came swinging forward, with her feet straight out in front of her. They neatly fit between the bars of the fire escape railing and they connected with Missy's shins.

"Aaauuuggghhh!" Missy went crashing down on the ground, her shins burning. Her back hit the stairs and she could feel the steel pressing into her backbone.

Mashela flipped over the bars and ran up the stairs, stepping on Missy's fingers in the process. The wound she earlier inflicted on Missy's thumb opened. Missy screamed again. For a moment she thought about praying, but her mind was too clouded with rage. She was angry...no... she was *mad*.

Suddenly Missy lost all fright about the situation and, against her better judgment, she began to run up the stairs after Mashela. Her steps were slow to begin with, but the adrenaline running through her numbed away the pain. Still...in the back of her mind, Missy could feel a numbness setting upon her heart.

She slowed down for a split second to consider, but all it took was watching Mashela run up the stairs with all her might. It gave Missy a feeling of power she hadn't felt before. It gave her a feeling of revenge.

Missy began to take the stairs two by two. Rapper was up to the fourth story already. He only had one more to go. If only he knew what was going on. If only he could help.

Missy couldn't understand the reason Mashela was running, but as she reached the fire escape base of the fourth story, she saw it. In the air, at the top of the building, it hovered. A Serfsled. The Academy's power went out before Alex could stop it from coming. It had arrived— and it was waiting for its passenger to take it home.

The Serfsled had two long seats, one in front of the other, positioned on top of polished, black rectangles housing the craft's air-compression engine. It was silent and used only air for fuel. The windshield at the front made it look somewhat like a motorcycle, but its clear base was wide and flat. It was the perfect getaway vehicle. But if Missy could help it, Mashela wouldn't get to try it out.

Missy shot forward and grabbed the back of Mashela's fluorescent-orange outfit. Mashela screamed as Missy caught a few strands of her hair at the same time. Mashela stopped running and, with Missy holding on tight, she began running *backward*. Missy shrieked. Rapper stopped. He moved his head around, but was still unaware of what was happening.

The NME agent slammed Missy back into the steel railing and a bolt, stuck into the concrete of the building's side, popped out. The railing shook. The platform shook. Mashela lurched forward again toward the top of the building, and Missy chased after her again.

"Stop!" she cried. Mashela didn't obey. Instead, when she reached the next platform, she whirled around on one foot and caught Missy in the stomach. Missy coughed as she dropped back down the stairs, reaching out for support. She hit the platform below with a thud that made another bolt pop out.

Missy's body rolled over the steel base. Suddenly the platform cracked away from the wall and tipped down. Missy's eyes widened. She grabbed for the grated bar and forced her fingers through its steelwork. She felt a jolt of gravity as she slipped over the side, but her fall was stopped by her finger hold. The stairway rocked gently. She let out a long, nervous breath. She had to get back up. She pulled. She stopped.

Mashela stood above her, sturdily, looking down at her. Mashela cracked a grin.

"You don't like the way I'm looking at you, do you?"

"What?!"

"I said, you don't like the way I'm looking at you, do you?"

"Actually, I'm a bit preoccupied with staying alive right now."

"Yeah?" Mashela pursed her lips and narrowed her eyes. "Well, maybe you'd better take a look, because I may be the last person you ever see. And I want you to look at my face. Look at the way I'm looking at you!"

Missy could feel a lump in her throat and a tear trying to squeeze out of her eye. It was cold, and the steel was colder. And her fingers were hurting...and she couldn't pull herself up with Mashela standing there, taunting her.

"Look at me!" Mashela shouted. Her loud voice jolted Missy. Missy looked into her rival's eyes. Was that a tear forming in *her* eye? Was that emotion on *her* face?

Missy couldn't take her eyes off Mashela's face. She felt that tear escape and run back into her hair. Her fingers burned.

"This is the face you have given me time and again," Mashela said coolly, pointing to her own countenance. "This is the face that says, 'I'm better than you because of where I'm standing.' Missy, this is *your* face."

"No...no...it's not..."

"Don't tell me it's not!" Mashela shouted. "I've seen it! This is the face you looked at me with every time you brought me food. You were so proud because you were on the other side of the bars. This is the face you wore whenever you talked about Paul—because you thought you knew him better than I did. This is the face you had on, Missy, just *five minutes ago*...when *I* was the one who seemed helpless. Funny...you're not wearing this face now."

"I know all about you, Mashela Knavery!" Missy shouted back, in a desperate attempt to change the topic. Her fingers were feeling numb. "I know you had a bad past, but God can change things for you like He did for me!"

Mashela's face softened a fraction and she swallowed hard. Her eyes reflected the sadness and emptiness she usually hid so well. "You're the one I don't understand," Mashela whispered. "You're so proud of who you are and what you've become, but you haven't shown me any good reason why I'd ever want your God."

The words smacked Missy in the face. Had she really been that proud? Worse yet...had she really been *that* unloving?

Mashela shook her head. "Those who show no mercy deserve no mercy," she whispered hoarsely. She lifted her foot. Missy looked at her own fingers. They were bright white.

"No-no! Please, no!"

Mashela's foot came down and Missy braced herself for the drop—but she never felt the impact.

Rapper knocked Mashela back, blindly, but effectively. She hit the ground with all her weight. Missy took the opportunity and pulled herself up. She pulled hand-over-hand up the grated surface and quickly came to rest. Rapper was leaning down toward her, hearing her short breaths. Missy reached up and grabbed the corner of the tape around his mouth.

*RRRRRRIIIIIIIIIPPPPPP!*

"Oooohhhhhhaaaaaaaaaaahhhhhhhhhh!" Rapper shouted in pain. "Augh! Did you have to pull so hard?! Get this blindfold off me so I can see!"

Missy reached up, but Mashela rebounded before she could get hold of the blindfold. Mashela looked down at Missy in disgust. She pushed Rapper hard and he bounded up the stairs as she shouted, "Go!"

As she left, she glanced back and shook her head at Missy, every muscle in her face whispering, *"Loser."*

Missy sat, defeated, hurting and tired. She watched Mashela lead Rapper the rest of the way up the fire escape in double time. Mashela's words lingered with her and dug deep into her heart. She knew deep down in there, there was a scripture or two she had learned about who she was in Christ and what He could do through her, but she couldn't think of them.

She felt alone.

She felt like her greatest treasure had been stolen—
her security.

"Oh, God," she prayed with a whimper, "please
show me what I've done wrong...I'm sorry for whatever
it is. Am I really the cruel person Mashela says I am?
Help me, please. I need help. I need help, in Jesus'
Name."

She looked up once more and could see Mashela
strapping Rapper into his place in the Serfsled. She was
going to get away. She was going to kidnap Rapper. It
was hard to stomach.

But suddenly something grabbed Missy's attention.
It was what glimmered in a drop of sunlight. It was on
Mashela's hand. It was the ring Paul had given her. The
ring that reminded her of her covenant relationship
with Paul.

Missy felt a surge of energy penetrate her bones.
Her rival was getting away with the one thing Missy
never really thought she could get...she was stealing
away Missy's brother/sister relationship with Paul. The
ring was the symbol, Missy's recent carelessness was
the truth of the matter. She couldn't let that happen. She
had to stop Mashela. She needed another chance.
Mashela wasn't gone yet...and if Missy had anything to
do with it, she was going to get that chance.

Missy jumped to her feet and ran up the remainder of the fire escape. She could still feel her bruised body aching from its connection with the cold, hard steel. Her fingers throbbed. Her thumb bled.

Commander Kellie's instructions had been clear. Top priority was saving Rapper—then stopping Mashela from escaping. As Missy drew closer, she kept her eye on the ring Paul had given her.

"Get away!" Mashela shouted as Missy closed in. She was running now, straight at Mashela. Rapper was fully strapped in the Serfsled, but was still unable to see anything or use his arms.

"Get away!" Mashela screamed again viciously.

Missy didn't listen to her. As far as she was concerned, two could play at Mashela's game. If it was a fight Mashela wanted, it was a fight Mashela would get. In the back of Missy's mind, she vaguely remembered something God's Word said about not battling with flesh and blood...but she couldn't put her finger on it.

As Mashela moved to jump onto the front of the Serfsled and take off, Missy took action. Missy knew she'd only have one opportunity. She could either go after Rapper *or* Mashela—but not both. Just one. *But if*

*I can just stop Mashela first,* Missy thought, *then Rapper won't be going anywhere.* It wasn't what her commander had ordered, but it made sense...and it was a way for Missy to get her ring back.

Missy leapt into the air.

Missy caught Mashela just as she was getting seated for takeoff. Mashela latched onto the handlebar on the front of the Serfsled, but couldn't stop from being caught by the force of the barreling Superkid. As Missy and Mashela tumbled over the vehicle, it turned over with them, floating in midair.

"Aauugghh!" Rapper shouted, strapped in the back and now upside down.

The two girls hit the smooth top of the Superkid Deployment Ramp.

"Is this more of that Christian love you were telling me about?" Mashela said through a clenched jaw. She shoved Missy off to the side.

"I'm trying to save a friend," Missy tried to explain, standing up wearily.

Mashela was already up. "Him?" she asked, motioning to Rapper with her head. Rapper was still upside down in the craft.

"Yeah, me!" Rapper answered with a shout.

"Yes, him!" Missy responded harshly.

Mashela glanced over at Rapper. "He has to go with me," she stated matter-of-factly. "Besides, I don't think he's what you really want."

Missy tried not to take her eyes off Mashela's, but she couldn't help but do it for a second. Her ring, tightly stuck on Mashela's finger, glistened even though the sun was still behind clouds. She looked at it. She looked back at Mashela's piercing gaze.

"You're wrong," Missy said plainly. She suddenly broke out in a run for the Serfsled. Mashela took off after her. Missy reached it first and grabbed Rapper's constraints. Mashela stopped running the moment she saw Missy take hold of them.

"You are not *even* going to release that belt, are you?"

"Rapper's coming with me!" Missy shouted.

"No, my dear," Mashela replied coolly, "if you release that belt, Rapper isn't going with anyone. His hands are tied and he'll fall flat on his head."

"She has a point," Rapper whispered up to Missy.

Missy let go.

"Besides," Mashela continued, "as I said, I don't think he's what you really want." Missy glanced down at the ring again, then quickly back at Mashela.

"What is it *you* want?" Missy asked her enemy.

The question caught Mashela off guard and made her smile.

"Well," she answered, "I'm sorry I haven't been very clear about this, but I think I just want to get out of here...with the Serfsled...with your tied-up friend...and with," Mashela held her right hand up to Missy's face, *"my* ring."

Missy could feel her blood boiling.

"After all," Mashela continued maliciously, "I knew Paul before you did."

"Listen, *dear*," Missy shot back, "that's all fine and dandy, but first, you're going to have to go through me."

"*'Fine and dandy?'*" Rapper repeated. "Missy, we gotta work on your comebacks."

Missy and Mashela ignored him. Mashela looked down the bridge of her nose at Missy. "Don't tempt me," she whispered.

"Oh, great," Rapper said.

The two girls stared at each other.

Missy blinked first. Mashela's right fist came straight forward, aiming to connect with Missy's jaw, but the Superkid ducked just in time. Missy jabbed her own fist into Mashela's stomach and Mashela bent in pain.

Shock smacked Missy in the face harder than Mashela ever could have. Missy looked at her own throbbing hand and realized this was the first time she had ever used it to strike another. Worse yet, part of her wanted to strike again. She grabbed her fighting hand with her other and cradled it like a baby. Something was wrong. This wasn't her. This wasn't her at all. This wasn't a Superkid.

Mashela staggered back and looked up at Missy in surprise. The last time Missy had run into her, it had been in defense of a friend...This time, to Mashela's surprise, it clearly wasn't.

The NME agent stared at Missy for a long moment and then, noticing Missy's own shock, she walked past her. She decided to let Missy have the round...but she was still planning to win the tournament.

Mashela reached up and tapped on one of the controls on the Serfsled, then rolled a smooth trackball on the console to the right. The vehicle spun 180 degrees and righted itself. Rapper huffed in relief.

"Thanks, Missy," he said.

"It's not Missy," Mashela welcomed.

"Oh, great."

Mashela hopped up on the Serfsled and punched in some coordinates. Currents of air began to flow through the vehicle's compressor and it silently took off. Missy snapped out of her stupor as she felt the vehicle whisk past her, brushing her skin with warm air. It flew away.

Suddenly Missy realized she had allowed Mashela to get away—and she'd allowed Rapper to be kidnapped. And if that wasn't enough, Mashela had stolen the one symbol Missy had of her covenant relationship with Paul.

Missy slapped on her ComWatch.

"Let him go!" Missy cried, shouting to Mashela.

Her enemy just laughed at her, using Rapper's ComWatch, still on her wrist.

As Mashela fled, Missy closed her eyes in defeat. What had she done? Worse yet, what had Mashela done? Thoughts clunked around Missy's mind like marbles in a plastic ball. *Who was to blame?*

She saw Mashela grabbing her hand the night before and sneakingly sliding off her ring. She could see Mashela dropping from the ceiling and hurting her and her friends. She could see Mashela's hateful face as Missy dangled from the fire escape...yet there was something about Mashela...a sadness...a hurting...a driving force to her fear, her pain, her hate.

Or was there? After all, look at all Mashela had done! *She* was the one causing the trouble. *She* was the one to blame. *She* started it!

*She started it!* And someone had to finish it. Maybe she deserved the punch Missy gave her. Maybe it knocked her pride down a bit. Missy began to imagine what she'd do if she had another chance.

Missy felt a soft breeze brush her face. She opened her eyes.

*Zzzzzzzzzoooooooooommmmmmm!*

Missy hit the deck as Mashela came screaming overhead on the Serfsled. Missy barely saved herself from a nasty blow to the face by the clear, flat base of the air-cycle.

With a heartbeat resembling a drum roll, Missy realized her second chance to retaliate had come to her.

Mashela was circling around again, ready to knock Missy out just for spite. In the distance, Missy could see her staring determinedly through the front windshield of the vehicle. Missy began to run as fast as she could to avoid another close hit. She headed for the single door on the far side of the ramp that led into the Academy.

Swiftly, Mashela was down upon her and Missy ducked and rolled. Mashela came around again. Before Missy could get up, Mashela swooped down. Missy rolled aside and the underside of the Serfsled scraped the ramp, making a sound like a screeching cat. As the Serfsled lifted up, Missy looked at the underside. Painted from one tip to the other was the deep, olive green and black symbol of the Vipers—a menacing snake with a flickering, red tongue.

Missy got up and decided against continuing her run for the door. She couldn't make it. Mashela was too fast. Mashela came toward her again, but this time when she dipped down, Missy was ready. The Superkid dodged to the side and then launched out with her left hand and fastened herself to Mashela's right hand. She could feel the ring beneath her fingertips. She threw her free hand over and clasped on with it, too. She wasn't going to let go. She had her rival...she had her ring.

The sudden, added weight to the Serfsled caused it to tilt and stop its fast path forward. Mashela spun it around with her free hand and rolled the trackball a few degrees to straighten it out. For a moment, she and Rapper were suspended in the air, held by Missy. Then, though it wasn't fast because of the weight, the sled began to move forward again. As it slowly gained momentum, Missy looked down the ramp and saw they had only about 100 feet before they would be off the runway...and off the building. She had to act fast.

*Bam!*

Commander Kellie, Paul, Valerie, Alex and Techno burst out of the single, side door and stopped cold when they saw Missy being dragged down the ramp. They were too far away to catch up to Missy now.

"Missy!" Commander Kellie cried. "Let go! That's an order!"

"Missy!" Paul shouted, surprised at the sight.

Missy felt the ring against her fingertips and tried to pull it off as she was dragged. "But I've got Mashela!" she shouted to the others.

Commander Kellie and the Superkids looked at each other.

"Is she serious?" Alex had to ask.

Mashela peered down at Missy. "Yeah, you just keep holding on," she spat.

"I'm not letting go till you hand over yourself, Rapper, this Serfsled *and* my ring!"

"You really feel like you're in a position to bargain, don't you?"

Missy looked up at Mashela's face. It was cold. Her eyes were unsympathetic. Her lips were tight. Her mouth was a frown. Missy found herself frowning. Anger built up in her being. She knew Mashela wanted her to die. Missy's hands tightened on Mashela's. She wasn't going to let go. She was going to win this rivalry.

Her hands kept tightening. Her knuckles, which hurt only moments earlier, didn't hurt now. Rage flowed through them. Her thumb didn't even hurt. She looked straight into Mashela's face. She had to let this girl know exactly how she felt.

"You!" Missy cried, frustrated. Mashela looked down at Missy. "Mashela Knavery!" she said her name as though it was bitter on her tongue. Then she let her have it. "I hate—"

"...of the cage! Missy!"

*What was...*

"Missy!"

It was Valerie.

"Missy!"

Her voice was full of urgency. Missy had never heard Valerie sound so sharp before.

"Missy!"

Missy turned her head to look at Valerie. She was far away with Paul, Alex, Techno and Commander Kellie... but Missy could hear her. She was saying...

"Missy! Get your hand out of the cage!"

Missy's throat went dry. She turned to look at her hands, clasped around Mashela's.

Like a monkey in Valerie's story, Missy had hold of the shiny bait...and she wasn't letting go.

"But I've forgiven Paul!" Missy shouted aloud, more at herself than anyone else. For the first time since her troublesome adventure had begun, Missy heard the voice of the Holy Spirit speaking to her loud and clear.

*Paul's not the one you're offended with,* He said.

"But who?" Missy wondered innocently as her eyes lifted and met Mashela's once again. The revelation hit her like a baseball connecting with a bat. As she stared into Mashela's eyes, she realized she had allowed Mashela to offend her. That offense had stolen God's Word from her heart. It had hindered her prayers. It had nearly cost Missy her life on more than one occasion.

Missy looked down at her hand again. It was holding her offense. She was the one in a cage now. A cage of sin. She had screamed, thrown a fit and allowed herself to slip into more sin...but she never let go.

As she was dragged farther, Missy turned over Mashela's hand in her own and looked one last time at the ring on Mashela's finger. It was time to let go of the offense. She looked back at Mashela's face. As their eyes met, Mashela's eyebrows twitched. She looked at Missy, questioning. Missy, suddenly oblivious to what was happening, bit her lip and felt her chin quiver. She whispered the words.

"I don't hate you. I won't hate you."

Mashela's mouth parted in astonishment. Suddenly, a tear crept out of her eye that she couldn't retract. It slid along her beautiful dark cheek and was swept off with the wind.

Missy smiled at her rival for the first time. In her heart, she forgave her and both girls could feel the evident love of God enveloping them. Mashela shook as a chill ran down her spine.

"No," she whispered.

Missy cocked her head in wonderment. "No?"

"No...I won't...I can't!" Mashela cried out. Missy didn't understand.

"I'm letting go," Missy whispered. She released her grasp.

"No!" Mashela shouted, grabbing onto Missy's hand. "No!"

The Serfsled was gaining momentum. They were drawing near to the edge of the building. Mashela suddenly had complete control...and for whatever reason, though Missy was pulling away, Mashela wouldn't let go.

The Serfsled pushed ahead. Missy had slowed it down, but its speed was gaining. Missy's feet periodically hit the top of the Superkid Deployment Ramp, tearing the soles of her shoes. While pulling away from Mashela, she tried to keep her feet pulled up at the same time. But with Mashela's unloosening grip around Missy's hands, it proved to be difficult.

The edge of the building drew closer.

Missy shouted out to Mashela. "You don't want to do this!"

"I have to do this!" Mashela cried back.

"I don't understand you!"

"You don't understand NME!"

The edge of the building was coming closer... and closer.

Missy braced herself for the feeling of nothing beneath her feet. She knew the moment they were clear of the ramp, Mashela would let go and she would fall. Missy didn't know what to do. She prayed in the spirit, knowing the Holy Spirit knew just what to pray. A solo thought ran through her mind about the peace she suddenly felt even in the middle of trouble. And then another about how love cast out her fear. Peace and courage were nowhere to be found when her hand was in the cage of offense. But they were with her now.

Missy saw the edge of the ramp rushing closer.

She closed her eyes.

She waited for Mashela to let go.

Suddenly the wind stopped.

Missy opened her eyes.

She looked up at Mashela, but her rival wasn't looking at her...she was looking at Missy's feet. Missy looked down and saw her feet were caught...by Techno. Paul was sitting on top of the shiny robot, smiling big.

"Paul!" Missy shouted. "You—"

"—came to rescue my covenant sister!" he completed her thought with a wide smile.

Mashela looked at him defiantly. Techno was whirring in the opposite direction, holding his ground. The Serfsled was still at the edge of the building, but not going over as long as Techno and Mashela held onto their common bond: Missy.

Paul looked up at Mashela. "What are you doin', Shea?" he asked. Disappointment reigned in his voice.

"You don't understand, Paul!" she shouted.

"What you're doing is *wrong*."

"You don't understand!"

"Try me."

Mashela huffed. "If I don't have a victory to report to NME, I can't go back," she spat through clenched teeth. "And there's a reason I must go back."

Paul looked at her and shook his head.

She explained. "I don't have a choice. You'd do the same thing in my shoes."

"I doubt that."

"Hey!" Rapper interrupted, still blindfolded. "You have me!" he shouted to Mashela. "Take me as your prize to NME—just let Missy go!"

"No, Rapper!" Missy cried.

"You're already spoken for!" Mashela yelled, glancing back at Rapper.

"You're in a lot of trouble, aren't you?" Missy challenged Mashela. The two girls' eyes connected once more.

"No..." Mashela whispered, suddenly blank. "Not me..."

"We can help you," Missy offered. Mashela shook her head.

"The last person I need help from is *you.*"

"But we're the same!" Missy shouted.

The shock on Mashela's face was evident. "'Scuse me?"

"You heard me. We're the same. Look at us!"

Mashela frowned.

"We have some obvious physical similarities," Missy explained. "For instance, we're both beautiful."

"Well, *one* of us is anyway," Mashela interjected spitefully.

"Thank you."

Mashela looked down at Missy. "I was talking about me." She smiled curtly. Missy smiled back.

"Look," Missy said pointedly, "we may be different people, but we have one thing in common you can't dispute—Jesus went to the cross for both of us, died and rose again so we could have life."

"You don't understand what I'm up against!"

"I'm not the one holding on to you, Mashela, you're holding on to me. And as long as you do, I have something to say. Jesus wants to be your Lord. He doesn't care what you're up against or what you've done. He wants you!"

"Why would He want me?" Mashela spat back.

The words came to Missy. "Because He loves you."

Missy knew it was the Holy Spirit speaking through her. She could hear Him clearly again, now that she had let go of the offense. He knew Mashela's past better than she or Paul ever would. And He knew just what Mashela needed to hear. He knew how to water the seeds that had been planted in her heart.

Mashela nodded in recognition—and that was it. After Missy told her the Lord loves her, she just nodded. Missy wasn't sure what it meant. Did she accept what the Holy Spirit was saying? Did she just not know what to say? Was she simply patronizing Missy? Whatever it meant, it was something. And it was the kindest action she'd given toward Missy yet.

Then she let go.

Mashela let go of Missy's hands and Paul lunged forward, grabbing Missy at the waist. Missy was suddenly jolted back into Paul's arms as Techno charged away.

Mashela and Rapper sped off the Superkid Deployment Ramp and shot off into the sky.

"They're getting away!" Missy shouted as Paul set her down. Commander Kellie and the Superkids finally reached her and Paul in the center of the ramp.

Commander Kellie thumped her ComWatch and shouted Mashela's name. Mashela looked in the ComWatch she'd stolen from Rapper. She shot the commander a defiant look.

"Want one last look at the winner?" she asked.

"No," Commander Kellie responded. "I just wanted you to have one last look at me."

"Huh?"

Swiftly, Commander Kellie pulled the Hi-lighter out of her uniform pant pocket and shot it directly into the ComWatch. In the distance, Missy saw the burst of blinding light hit Mashela in the eyes. The Serfsled twisted its course like a writhing snake as Mashela wrenched to regain control.

Commander Kellie turned off her ComWatch. "I imagine she'll fly blind for a few hours, but at least now she won't see where the Academy is located."

"But what about Rapper?" Missy said through teary eyes. "We have to do something!"

Commander Kellie bit her lip and looked at Missy sadly. She grabbed her hand and held it tight. "What we can do now is pray for him, Missy," she said softly. "Mashela disrupted our entire communications system while she was in Sub-Level 3. Until it's fixed, we're grounded."

"That's why it took so long for us to get up here," Alex explained. "She electronically sealed all the doors and express lifts."

Missy felt her lips quivering. She looked at Mashela disappearing into the sky. Then she looked over at her best friend, Valerie.

"I can't believe I let myself get offended at Mashela," she admitted as her voice broke. "I nearly lost my life and I nearly let Mashela discover the Academy's location and—my offense caused us to lose Rapper."

"I know," Commander Kellie said, giving Missy a warm hug, "but we forgive you...and I know Rapper does, too."

Paul nodded. "If I know Rapper, he can hold his own. He'll be all right."

"Yes, he will," Valerie agreed. "Let's pray for him now."

Commander Kellie and the Superkids grabbed hands.

▲　▲　▲

Missy, feeling bruised and aching, was scrubbing away at one of 47, deeply stained Academy outfits. It was a job that had to be done, but no one had been available to do it. Until now. Today, as part of Missy's correction for disobedience, she was put on disciplinary duty for four weeks. No adventures, no special events, no fun. During training hours, she would continue to attend classes, but during her free time, she was to stay at the Academy...and since she was there, she was kept busy with projects that had lagged behind. It was work, but Missy understood why it was *her* work. After being given a short time to recover, she had now been given plenty of time to think.

Missy stood at a square, shiny metal washbasin at the far end of Superkid Academy's basement laundry room. Surrounding her were stacks of neatly folded towels, baskets of dingy workout clothes with individuals' names neatly stitched on them, and several super-capacity cleaning units. As Missy scrubbed, she thought about what she had said to Mashela at the very end—that they were both the same. Jesus had died and risen again for both of them. But Missy was the only one of the two who had accepted His cleansing...so far.

It struck Missy as odd that Mashela would actually want to live day after day wearing her old, dirty life when God has something so much better for her. For some reason, Mashela had a hard time understanding that. It was like she thought God didn't have any new lives in her size.

But Missy didn't feel like one to preach. She had dirtied her new life by playing in the grime of offense. She muddied her judgment and dirtied her example.

Thank God, His forgiveness is a washing machine, always ready for a new load. Missy hoped Mashela had seen that, too. She wondered if she did. She remembered the nod Mashela had given her when Missy had told her the Lord loves her...but Missy still wasn't sure what the nod had meant. Maybe she had broken through, maybe not. But the Word was still given and it couldn't be taken away. Like Isaiah 55:11 says, His Word will achieve its purpose.

"Hi, Missy."

The greeting startled Missy, but she smiled when she saw the greeter. Commander Kellie was wearing a casual outfit: tapered, black slacks, a long-sleeved, dark green knit shirt and black ankle boots. Her dark brown hair was down and small, emerald earrings set in silver peeked out when she tipped her head.

"Hello, Commander," Missy said politely. She didn't stop scrubbing.

"How are you doing?" Commander Kellie asked. Her hazel eyes searched Missy's. Missy looked down at the deep stain on the uniform from the Yellow Squad she was working on. She took a deep breath.

"Well," Missy replied, "out of 47, I only have about 42 more to go. These yellow ones are especially feisty."

Commander Kellie laughed. She touched Missy's shoulder. "No, I mean how are *you* doing."

Missy turned off the warm, pouring water and set the yellow uniform down in the sink. Resident water collected in its folds. She wiped her hands on the closest wrinkled towel.

"I just can't believe I messed up so badly. I'm not that kind of person."

Commander Kellie nodded lightly. "Look at the positive side, Missy. If you hadn't listened to the Holy Spirit and let go of that offense when you did, we might have lost you, too. You're right—taking offense was definitely wrong. But if you hadn't let go of the offense, the devil could have really done some bad things."

Missy nodded. "Can I ask you a question, though, Commander Kellie?"

"Of course, Missy."

"Well..." Missy looked down into the basin. The ceiling light reflected in the metal. "I guess I just don't understand why what I did wrong had to affect Rapper—and could have affected you all! I mean, I guess I feel I deserved whatever was coming to me...but why did something have to happen to Rapper?"

Commander Kellie leaned against a smooth, steel table. "Me, you, Rapper—we're all individuals, but Ephesians 4 also says that we are one body in Christ. What one of us does or doesn't do affects the rest of us. We're only as strong as our weakest link: That's why we must build each other up in the Lord. We need each other."

"Leave it to me to prove it."

Commander Kellie smiled. Missy decided to change the subject.

"So are our communications systems back online?" Missy asked.

"They are," the Commander reported. "Alex and Techno found the section of transfers Mashela interrupted and reinstated the links. That's something interesting—Alex said she could have caused some serious trouble and shut down the Academy for weeks...but she apparently chose not to. There's a lot more to Mashela than meets the eye."

"I think so, too. In the middle of our struggle, she said a few things that made it sound like NME was holding something over her head. I wonder what they have over her that's so strong she's willing to do whatever they say—even hurt someone like she did me...or worse. Do you think we'll ever find out?"

"I pray so...but one thing's for sure: I don't think we've seen the last of Mashela Knavery."

Missy closed her eyes as her stomach turned. "I just feel awful about Rapper," she stated, not able to let the subject go quite yet.

"Rapper's going to be all right," Commander Kellie reassured her, squeezing her shoulders.

"You know where he is?"

"We're working on it. There's no telling what twists and turns she made while flying blindly. But once her sight returns, she'll figure out her location and head to the nearest city. We'll have scouts in every one of them."

Suddenly the thin door to the laundry area sprang open. Paul entered with an armful of white chef's uniforms. "Incoming!" he cried.

Commander Kellie squeezed Missy's shoulders again. She winked reassuringly at Missy and then said hello to Paul as she passed him on the way to the door.

"Oh, sorry. I didn't mean to interrupt," he said.

Commander Kellie shook her head. "No interruption—I was just leaving." She headed out the door.

"Look what I have for you!" Paul said, pushing the clump of chefs' uniforms into Missy's hands. "As you know, they served spaghetti for lunch—with plenty of thick, red sauce."

Missy thumbed through the uniforms. "One, two, three...four, five. Now I have 47 again." She sighed.

The room was suddenly awkwardly silent. Missy put the chefs' outfits aside and reached for the scrubber again. She watched Paul out of the corner of her eye and wondered what he was thinking.

"I meant what I said," he voiced. The words hung in the room. Missy rolled the scrubbing sponge around in her hand.

"About what?" she questioned lightly. She wanted to make sure she wasn't putting any pressure on Paul if he was talking about what she thought he was talking about. She wanted him to say it himself...because he *wanted* to say it.

Paul smirked and looked into the distance. He shook his head and looked down at the floor. Missy tried to hide her smile. She eyed him smartly, her whole face asking the question, *So are you going to come out with it?*

"You know about what," Paul responded, looking up at her.

Missy considered his words then folded her arms across her chest. "No, I don't know about what," she said, a bit feisty.

"I meant what I said about being your covenant brother."

Missy smiled.

"Now, I don't consider that a light thing," Paul informed her. "I wouldn't just go around and become a covenant brother with just anyone I meet. I mean, it doesn't mean I'll be your covenant brother this week and not the next—it means I'm part of your family and you're part of mine...though I don't really have one. But what does belong to me is yours and vice versa. Since our parents were covenant partners it makes sense. Because, you know, I wouldn't just—"

Paul was interrupted by a sudden hug from Missy. He hugged her back. A short moment later, they both let go.

"Well," Missy stated, not sure what to say next.

"Well," Paul repeated, straightening the collar on his rugby.

"I, uh, I don't suppose we'll talk about this a whole lot in the future, huh?"

"Knowing us, probably not," Paul admitted.

Missy rubbed her right ring finger.

"Paul, I'm sorry Mashela stole my ring. I really didn't mean to lose it."

"I've been thinking about that and you know, I don't think she took it just to escape from her cell...or even just for spite."

"You don't?"

"I have a feeling she wanted it...you know, to try and regain some of who she used to be."

"That's deep, Paul."

"Hey, I'm a deep kinda guy."

Missy giggled. "Oh, brother."

"Don't concern yourself over the ring," he added. "It's just a 'thing.' The covenant relationship I have with your family is the real promise."

"All riiiight," Missy said smoothly, knocking her fist against Paul's. Paul turned and exited the room.

Missy stood still and silent for the first time in a long time. She looked down into the shiny, metal bin. She could see her face, blurred, looking back at her. A tight knot formed in her throat as she peered into her own eyes and saw how true those words the Holy Spirit had spoken through her were. She remembered her dream. Yes, Mashela's eyes were her own.

A broken breath escaped from Missy's lips as she cleared a space on the floor beneath her. Slowly, she sat down on the hard, laundry room floor. She curled up her legs and hugged them, leaning back against a leg of a table. She dropped her forehead to her knees.

"I'm sorry," she whispered, unintelligibly to even her own ears. "Jesus, I've never been so scared as I was around Mashela."

The warm wetness of tears soaked into her pant leg. "God, I never want to be without Your anointing again. I was so scared. I felt like I had nothing without You there...I realize how much I need You."

Missy let out a long, wavering breath. She pulled her head up. "I never want to be offended again. I never want to feel like that again. I won't stop praying for Mashela. I won't. And I won't stop praying for Rapper. And..."

Missy leaned her head back against the hard, metal table leg. "Father, You're so good to me...I've done all this...and yet...You still honor me with my desire to have a brother. Your mercies really don't ever end..."

Sitting silently, Missy stared ahead at her own eyes, reflected in the metal side of the washbin. In them, she could see Mashela. She could see Paul. She could see the world.

Time passed slowly. When her hands stopped shaking, Missy arose and decided she needed to stay

busy if she was to finish the washing before midnight.
She turned the water on again and picked up a stained,
yellow uniform. She wiped her eyes with the back of her
free hand and swallowed hard. She could feel the peace
of the Holy Spirit surrounding her, comforting her.

Diligently, she began to scrub away the grime, and
as she did, she spoke out Bible verses she had stored in
her heart. It was good to know they were still there.
Soon, she began to sing some praise songs, too, stirring
herself up with the Word. Getting offended, she
decided, was just never worth it. Instead, from now on,
she would take up the Sword of the Spirit—God's
Word—and the Shield of Faith. After all, the Superkid
concluded, the best way to keep from a bad offense is
with a good defense.

After flying for more than four hours, Rapper's backside was aching. The Serfsled seat was less than comfortable and his riding companion had stayed silent the entire time. Rapper turned his thoughts to prayer when Mashela suddenly said:

"Good."

"Good?" Rapper echoed, happy to know she was conscious. "What good?"

"My eyesight's coming back. The blurs are turning to shapes."

"Must be nice to be able to see."

"I'm not taking off your blindfold."

"I know."

Twenty minutes passed before Mashela spoke up again. "Great."

"Great?" Rapper echoed. "What great?"

"We're way off course."

"I'm just glad we haven't hit a tree."

"You're such a wimp. I've kept us high in the sky."

"Then I'm glad we didn't hit a skyscraper."

Mashela huffed.

Rapper continued, "Are you going to give me my ComWatch back?"

"I tossed that primitive technology off my arm an hour ago," Mashela said coolly. "I don't need your so-called friends tracking me."

"You can't track someone by their ComWatch," Rapper said flatly. As if she was telling him the truth anyway. For all he knew she was holding the watch in front of his face.

With the midafternoon sun, the air had become warmer. More time passed and the wind shifted direction as Mashela found her course. With his thoughts, Rapper prayed, believing Psalm 91:3, that God was his Deliverer. Finally, Rapper couldn't help but ask the question that had been nagging at him for the past several hours. "So what did you mean, I'm 'spoken for'?"

"What?"

"You said to Missy that I was spoken for. What'd you mean by that? You going to bring me back to the Vipers?"

"Now there's an interesting idea. Send you into a den of wolves."

"No thanks," Rapper said.

"You don't get a vote," Mashela retorted. Then, "But that's not where you're going, no."

"Back to NME then? As your prisoner?"

There was a long pause before Mashela responded, "NME has enough prisoners."

"So then what—"

"I'm sorry," Mashela interrupted. "What was it I did that made you think I wanted conversation?"

"Oh, no, *I'm* sorry," Rapper said. "What was it *I* did that made you think I wanted to be kidnapped?'

Mashela didn't say a word, but Rapper could tell she wasn't exactly warming up to him.

Another undeterminable amount of time passed. And time and again, he pulled at the duct tape binding his wrists together, but couldn't stretch it.

"You know you're a lousy conversationalist anyway," Rapper said after he was tired of struggling.

*Whap!*

The back of Mashela's hand struck Rapper in the mouth.

"Ow! Hey!" Rapper shouted. And without thinking, his foot shot forward and kicked his captor in the ankle.

"That's it," Mashela said. Suddenly Rapper heard a click. Then his seat belt unfastened.

"What are you doing?!" the Superkid cried.

"Taking out the trash," said Mashela. And with a sharp flip of the Serfsled, Rapper was suddenly free falling through the air.

Blindfolded.

With his arms tied behind his back.

*Where's a good parachute when you need one?*

## To be continued...

After being dropped headfirst
into a **junkyard** mystery—
Rapper discovers the one thing
he must never **throw away.**

Look for *Commander Kellie and the Superkids*<sub>SM</sub>
novel #6—

# Mystery of the Missing Junk

**by Christopher P.N. Maselli**

## Prayer for Salvation

Father God, I believe that Jesus is Your Son and that You raised Him from the dead for me. Jesus, I give my life to You. Right now, I make You the Lord of my life and choose to follow You forever. I love You and I know You love me. Thank You, Jesus, for giving me a new life. Thank You for coming into my heart and being my Savior. I am a child of God! Amen.

## About the Author

Christopher P.N. Maselli is the author of the *Commander Kellie and the Superkids* Adventure Series. He also writes the bimonthly children's magazine, *Shout! The Voice of Victory for Kids,* and has contributed to the *Commander Kellie and the Superkids* movies.

Originally from Iowa and a graduate of Oral Roberts University, Chris now lives in Fort Worth, Texas, with his wife, Gena, where he is actively involved in the children's ministry at his local church. When he's not writing, he enjoys in-line skating, playing computer games and collecting Legos.

# Other Books Available

Baby Praise Board Book
Baby Praise Christmas Board Book
Noah's Ark Coloring Book
The Best of *Shout!* Adventure Comics
The *Shout!* Joke Book
The *Shout!* Super-Activity Book

## *Commander Kellie and the Superkids*<sub>SM</sub> **Books:**

*The SWORD Adventure Book*
*Commander Kellie and the Superkids*<sub>SM</sub> *Series*
    Middle Grade Novels by Christopher P.N. Maselli

    #1 *The Mysterious Presence*
    #2 *The Quest for the Second Half*
    #3 *Escape From Jungle Island*
    #4 *In Pursuit of the Enemy*
    #5 *Caged Rivalry*
    #6 *Mystery of the Missing Junk*

# World Offices
## of Kenneth Copeland Ministries

For more information about KCM and a free
catalog, please write the office nearest you:

Kenneth Copeland Ministries
Fort Worth, Texas 76192-0001

Kenneth Copeland
Locked Bag 2600
Mansfield Delivery Centre
QUEENSLAND 4122
AUSTRALIA

Kenneth Copeland
Post Office Box 15
BATH
BA1 3XN
ENGLAND U.K.

Kenneth Copeland
Private Bag X 909
FONTAINEBLEAU
2032
REPUBLIC OF SOUTH AFRICA

Kenneth Copeland
Post Office Box 378
Surrey
BRITISH COLUMBIA
V3T 5B6
CANADA

UKRAINE
L'VIV 290000
Post Office Box 84
Kenneth Copeland Ministries
L'VIV 290000
UKRAINE